Edward Sylvester Ellis

The Fugitives
The Quaker Scout of Wyoming

ISBN/EAN: 9783337412272

Printed in Europe, USA, Canada, Australia, Japan

Cover: Foto ©Andreas Hilbeck / pixelio.de

More available books at **www.hansebooks.com**

Edward Sylvester Ellis

The Fugitives

The Quaker Scout of Wyoming

OR,

THE QUAKER SCOUT OF WYOMING

By EDWARD S. ELLIS,

AUTHOR OF "SETH JONES," "FRONTIER ANGEL," "BILL BIDDON," ETC

LONDON:

GEORGE ROUTLEDGE & SONS,

THE BROADWAY, LUDGATE.

THE FUGITIVES.

CHAPTER I.

THEY COME!

" THE Indians are coming ! The Indians are coming !"
was the terrified exclamation of Gershom Smithson, as he
came thundering down the road, on a hot day in July,
from Forty Fort, in Wyoming Valley. He was mounted
without a saddle on a coal-black steed that was under full
gallop; the long yellow hair of the rider streamed in the
wind thus created, his whole countenance indicative of
the most extreme excitement. At intervals he glanced
furtively behind him, and then, pounding his heels against
the foaming sides of his horse, dashed forward at the same
tremendous rate. That mild summer sky was obscured
by the smoke of battle and burning houses, and the air
resounded with the desultory rattle of musketry, the
shouts of the vanquished settlers, and the yells of the tri-
umphant Indians.

" It's all up !" he muttered; "and every man must
look out for himself and folks. Too bad ! too bad ! This
is a dark day for the Valley."

At the roadside he discerned a mother, two daughters,
and a small boy, standing in front of their dwelling,
watching and waiting with the most acute apprehension
for tidings of the battle.

" Fly ! fly for your lives !" he called, as he reined up
his horse.

" Are we defeated ?" asked the mother, coming forward, her face white, and her whole frame quivering with terror.

" Yes ; completely routed and driven back ! We went out and attacked Butler and his Indians, but they over-whelmed us."

" And where is John and Willie ?"

" Were your husband and son in the fight ?"

" Yes—both went."

" God knows whether they're living or dead. Our line was thrown into confusion and the Indians are massa-cring every one in their hands. It's no place here for you ; they'll soon be along this way."

" But—how did you escape ?"

" When I found it was all up, I made for the woods. Before I knowed it, I found a big red-skin on a horse trying to run me down. When we got into the woods I dropped him, and this is his animal."

" Where are you going ?"

" To 'tend to the old woman and little one. They live a half-mile up the road. Come, you're losing precious time."

" But, oh ! where shall we go ?"

" Anywhere—away from here."

" But where ; in what direction ?"

" Toward Wind Gap or Stroudsburg."

" Oh ! my husband ! my husband ! my darling Willie ! what will become of us ?"

Gershom Smithson dashed a tear from his eye.

" It's hard—mighty hard—I know ; but it can't be helped. They may escape. When I left, the most of them were running for Monocacy Island. I must be off, or the old woman will give me up."

The rider gave his steed the rein, and went tearing down the road at a tremendous gait. The alarm by this time was becoming general, and the women and children were beginning to crowd the roads and paths in the woods —all fleeing in abject terror from a foe that knew no mercy. Fitful discharges of guns in every direction, the palpable smell of gunpowder and smoke in the air, the occasional glimpses of the seething flame in the valley, all spoke of the terrible scenes that were being enacted in that beautiful spot on the Susquehanna. Shouts, screams, and rifle reports were heard from every quarter—betraying the fact that the settlers were hopelessly defeated and were fleeing blindly to every point that offered the least chance of escape.

Smithson, or, as he was generally termed, " old Gershom," had ridden scarcely a hundred rods when he encountered a woman carrying an infant, with two small children clinging to her dress. He recognized her instantly as the wife of a man that had been shot and tomahawked by his side less than an hour before. His heart bled with pity, and he would have gladly yielded up his animal to them were there not stronger claims upon him in the person of his own wife and infant.

" Whoa ! is that you, Mrs. Ogden ?"

" Yes ; our men have been driven back, hav'n't they ?"

" Yes ; the whole Valley is thrown open, and the Indians are over-running us."

" Did you see anything of Joseph ?"

" Make all haste to the Wind Gap ; for they will cut off every fugitive they can reach," replied the old man, evading the question.

" Oh, Gershom ! you were in the same company with Joseph. Do you know anything about him ?"

" I saw him retreating—"

" Ah ! you saw more yet.   It is in your face ; don't deceive me ; anything is better than suspense.   Did he fall?"

" Yes," answered Smithson, reluctantly.

" Dead?"

" I am afraid so; he was shot."

" Can he still be living ?"

" No ; I saw him killed."

" God's will be done !" gasped the widow.

" He died like a brave man with his face to the foe, and there's many a gallant fellow to keep him company."

" I may as well sit down and die, for I care nothing about living now," wailed the widow, in despair.

" But your children ?"

" Yes ; for them I will press on.   I have a brother at Stroudsburg.   I will make all haste there."

" Mrs. Ogden, I would give you my horse, but Jerusha and the baby are waiting for me.   Keep up a good heart ; we must all die some day, and don't let us cry if it comes sooner than we expect."

Once more Gershom Smithson struck his horse into a gallop.   Surely time was precious, and he began to be apprehensive that his wife, who was a muscular, strong-minded woman, had joined the other fugitives that had taken the alarm.

" Just like Jerusha," he soliloquized.   " If she thought the baby was in danger she wouldn't wait a minute—Holloa !"

He was now passing through a thick piece of woods, and his exclamation was caused by the sharp crack of a rifle, a few rods in advance.   Not knowing exactly how to take this, he drew his horse down to a walk, and cocked his rifle, to which he had persistently clung all day. While thus gazing forward, he saw a man, bareheaded, barefooted, bleeding and panting, his arms hanging down as if perfectly helpless, run wearily across the road, and glancing with a wild look of alarm behind him, plunge into the forest upon the other side. He seemed to be ready to drop from exhaustion, and, it was manifest, could continue his flight but a short distance further. He did not observe "old Gersh," who pulled his horse to one side, so as not to attract attention, and calmly awaited the *dénoûment*.

"If that man's running, there's some one chasing; and if there's any one chasing that poor half-dead soldier, it's a red-skin—and if it's a red-skin, why here's a man that's going to have something to say in the matter."

The words were yet in the mouth of the horseman, when a Delaware Indian, in his war-paint, and bearing both a rifle and tomahawk, bounded into the road, and with his basilisk eyes fixed upon the spot where the fugitive had disappeared, leaped like a blood-hound after him. His indurated muscles made him apparently as fresh and agile as ever. Like the white man he failed to observe the horseman, and had already reached the opposite side of the road, when the latter gave utterance to a peculiarly wild whoop. As quick as lightning the Delaware turned his startled glance up the road. As he did so he saw the black horse, with flashing eyes, erect ears, and expanded nostrils, standing as motionless as a statue, while, rising just above his head, was visible the sallow face, long yellow hair, broad-brimmed hat and gleaming eyes of Gershom Smithson. Scarcely two inches above the horse's head and directly between his ears, rested his long rifle, pointing straight as the finger of Fate at the head of the Indian.

The latter had barely time to see his danger, when "old Gersh's" finger pressed the trigger, and the pistol-like crack of the piece and the death-shriek of the savage were almost simultaneous.

"I jes' yelped, so as to make you turn your head, and giv' me a chance to take you between the eyes," he muttered, as he coolly proceeded to reload his gun. "It's my private opinion you won't hunt any more poor wounded soldiers, or tomahawk any women. That chap is clear of *you* at least."

He struck his horse into an easy canter, and bestowed only a contemptuous glance upon the human being that had just fallen by his hand.

"Would to heaven I could only serve you all in the same expeditious manner. You're making widows by the dozen."

This incident occasioned the old man more anxiety than anything that had occurred since his flight. It could not be doubted that the merciless hordes of Brandt were pressing eagerly upon the settlement, but he had not believed it possible that any of them could have reached this point as soon as this. He himself had come from the battle-field almost as fast as his horse could carry him, but he was behind this savage.

"It beats all natur'!" he muttered, "how that Indian travelled so far. This is a little too close to the old cabin to suit me."

His face showed his perplexity, and once more he put his horse to a full gallop. A short distance ahead, he turned at an abrupt angle, and riding through a sort of bridle-path, came upon a small cabin, such as is frequently constructed by the early settlers in a country. A large, bony woman, with an expression of impatience on her countenance, stood in the doorway, holding a small child.

"Where under the sun have you been all this time, Gersh!"

"In the battle, of course.'"

"Little good you did, I'll warrant. 'Pears to me you must have fought a good time."

"We did, Jerusha; but we got licked almost right away—"

"And as soon as you found yourself licked, why didn't you start home? You allers was such a fool, that you didn't know nothin'. I don't see what you let 'em lick you for, anyway. I'll warrant you I wouldn't, if I'd been there."

"Why, Jerusha, you shouldn't talk so. If you'd seen the sights that I've just seen, and that are going on now, you'd never speak a cross word again. The Indians are raging through the valley now, and—"

"Where'd you get that hoss?"

"I shot a savage that tried to kill me. Did you hear a gun go off just now?"

"I heerd suthin' crack."

"I dropped another that was after a white man. We must leave at once for Stroudsburg, for they'll soon be along this way."

"You goin' to carry us on that animal?"

"Yes; and you're luckier than the others around you."

Smithson dismounted, and assisted his wife to mount behind him. Thowing a bag of meal and some bread and meat across the horse, he was about to gallop off, when he paused. "It don't seem right for me to go off this way, when there are so many that need my help. Do you

s'pose you could get along without me, Jerusha, if I
should stay ? "

" Get along without you ? Of course, I can—and a
plaguy sight better than with you. I'd allers been better
off if I'd never see'd Gersh Smithson."

" I will stay, then. There's the Abingdon's that'll
need help, I think. You've been to Stroudsburg before;
just take the straight road."

" Oh, keep still ! Don't you s'pose I know the way as
well as you do ? Don't try to tell me anything."

" All right; farewell, dearest Jerusha; take good care
of yourself. I'll try and join you."

" Humph ! you needn't hurry," growled the wife, as she
turned her horse's head toward the main road. Her husband watched her fondly for a moment, and was about to
turn toward the residence of the Abingdon's, when his
spouse stopped the animal with a spiteful jerk.

" Gersh ! Gersh ! "

" What is it, dear Jerusha ? "

" Come here ! I tell you ! "

The obedient husband was by her side in a moment.

" You go in the house—up-stairs—in the closet—in the
bedroom—there you'll find my camfire-bottle. Bring it
here."

It required the obedient husband but a few moments
to obey this command; and fully satisfied, his wife rode
deliberately away, without exchanging another word.

" There goes a genius ; she'll take care of herself, and
the baby, as well as if I were with her. Ah ! me ! it's a
dreadful time ! I must hurry to the Abingdons."

Still communing with himself, he entered the wood,
and his rapid strides soon carried him beyond the sight of
his humble cabin.

CHAPTER II.

WYOMING'S SWEET VALE.

EARLY in the spring of 1778, the inhabitants of Wyoming Valley learned of a contemplated incursion in their settlement by the English and Indians. Their position was one of peculiar exposure, as very nearly all their able-bodied men were absent in the Continental army. Wyoming was the only considerable post above the Blue Ridge, and could this be desolated, the German settlements below the mountains were laid open to the fury of the different tribes.

Sensible of the dreadful danger, that every week was becoming more and more threatening, General Schuyler addressed the Board of War. The officers and men earnestly remonstrated that their families, left defenceless, were now menaced with invasion, and adverted to their terms of enlistment. But Congress seemed impervious to their pleadings, and refused to extend its helping hand until the middle of March, when it " Resolved, that one full company of foot be raised in the town of Westmoreland, on the east bank of the Susquehanna, for the defence of the said town, and the settlements on the frontiers, and in the neighbourhood thereof, against the Indians and the enemies of these States; the said company to be enlisted to serve one year from the time of their enlisting, unless sooner discharged by Congress."

This was an extraordinary resolution, as it is impossible to understand how a company, to be enlisted from among its inhabitants, could add to the strength of Westmoreland, and when, as has been remarked, nearly all her able-bodied men were absent in the army, and there was scarcely time to drill and discipline those that remained.

Furthermore, the resolution provided that the company find their own arms, accoutrements, and blankets. Here was another obstacle, almost insurmountable, as the valley had already been drained of its supplies. But the inhabitants, finding that God and their own strong arms were to be their reliance, set bravely to work to make ready for the blow that was now certain to come.

In the month of May, scouting parties encountered those of the enemy, at a distance of less than twenty miles from the settlement. They seemed merely out for information, as there were no murders or ravages committed. Shots were exchanged, but no one was injured, as the enemy seemed rather anxious to avoid battle. William Crook, coming out of an abandoned house, was shot dead in the door. This was the first man killed in Westmoreland by the Indians.

A few days later, a party of six men, on duty, were fired upon, one of their number killed, and another wounded. These incidents added to the alarm that was already distracting the settlements; but another occurrence took away the last spark of hope that may have remained in many breasts, for it proved beyond all possibility of doubt that the invasion was determined upon, and was shortly to be undertaken.

Two Indians, who were well known in Wyoming, from having dwelt there before, came down with their squaws on a visit, professing the warmest friendship. Suspicion arose that they were spies, and directions were given carefully to watch them. An old friend of theirs gained their confidence, and gave them drink after drink of rum, until they were stupidly drunk, when he gained from them the avowal that his people were preparing to cut off the settlement, the attack was to be made soon, and they had been sent down to examine and report how matters were. The two Indians were arrested and confined in Forty Fort, while their squaws were sent away.

The people in the outer settlements fled to the forts, and the wives of the soldiers sent messages, calling upon them by every tie to come home and protect them. Still, Congress and Connecticut (which at this time claimed jurisdiction from having sent most of the emigrants to Westmoreland), refused to allow the companies to depart. On learning the state of things, the companies became nearly disorganized. Every commissioned officer but two resigned, and more than twenty-five men deserted, and hastened to the assistance of the Valley. Among the latter was Gresham Smithson.

Finally, seven days before the battle, Congress interposed, and ordered that two companies already raised should be consolidated. This was intended to give the settlement something over a hundred men. They were directed to march to Lancaster, and shortly after (but too late) to Wyoming.

It soon became known that the enemy were concentrating at Newtown and Tioga, and preparing boats and canoes, whereupon all the men in the Valley capable of bearing arms were called out and drilled. The forts became filled with women, and every company was ordered to be ready at a moment's warning. A four-pounder was in Wilkesbarre Fort, but, as there was no ball, it was kept merely as an alarm gun.

The enemy, numbering four hundred British provincials, consisting of Colonel John Butler's Rangers, a detachment of Sir John Johnson' Royal Greens, the remainder being Tories from Pennsylvania, New Jersey, and New York, together with about seven hundred Indians, having descended the Susquehanna from Tioga Point, landed just below the mouth of Bowman's Creek on the west side of the river, about twenty miles above the Valley. Securing their boats, they marched across the peninsula, and arrived on the western mountain early on the morning of June 30th. Fort Jenkins, the uppermost fort in the Valley, was attacked in the morning. The garrison was small, but they fought bravely, and yielded only when literally overwhelmed.

This incident opened the campaign. Colonel Zebulon Butler, who chanced to be at home, by common consent assumed command of the Connecticut people. He sent out a party to bring in the dead bodies at Fort Jenkins. They were found scalped and shockingly mutilated. Two Indians near by, who were watching for any that might come to claim their friends, were both shot. One of the savages slain was shot by Zebulon Marcy, who was way-laid and hunted for years afterward by a brother of the Indian.

After the return of Colonel Z. Butler, Colonel John Butler took possession of Fort Wintermoot, which had been treacherously constructed by the Wintermoots for the benefit of the British.

On the same night a party was sent to reduce Fort Jenkins, whose garrison numbered seventeen old men. Four were slain, three made prisoners, when, there being no means of resistance left, the rest capitulated.

Early on the next morning, one of the prisoners, under the escort of a white man and an Indian, was sent to Colonel Zebulon Butler, demanding the surrender of Forty Fort and the Valley. A council of war was convened, which discovered a diversity of views. The leading officers were of the opinion that the best plan would be to procure a little delay, as it was supposed that Captain Spalding and his company were on their way; and, strengthened by such reinforcements, they were confident of repelling the invaders. The other party showed conclusively that while it was extremely doubtful of Captain Spalding's arrival, it was in the power of the enemy to desolate the Valley piecemeal. Two forts had already surrendered, and the Indians were already devastating exposed houses and families. So great was the individual anxiety of the men becoming for their families, that unless some decisive action was soon taken, each would rush to the protection of his own family.

As this was the sentiment of the majority, the minority reluctantly consented, and about the middle of the afternoon of that memorable 3rd of July, 1778, the column, consisting of three hundred men, old men, and boys, marched from the fort. They were divided into six regular companies. Among them were the judges of the court, all the civil officers far and near, grandfathers, and boys from fourteen to sixteen years of age.

Every movement of Colonel Z. Butler was vigilantly watched by his wary foe. Scarcely had he begun to march, when the intelligence was communicated to Colonel J. Butler, at Wintermoot's, who instantly sent word to the party at Fort Jenkins to hasten down and participate in the impending battle.

In approaching the enemy, Colonel Z. Butler (who is said to have been a distant relative of the British colonel), sent forward four of his officers to select the spot, and mark off the ground on which to form an order of battle. On coming up, the column deployed to the left, and by direction each company took its station, and then advanced in line to its proper position, when it halted. Everything was judiciously disposed, and conducted in a strictly military manner.

"Men, yonder is the enemy," said Colonel Butler. "The fate of your friends tells us what we have to expect if defeated. We come out to fight, not only for liberty, but for life itself, and what is dearer, to preserve our homes from conflagration, our women and children from the tomahawk. Stand firm the first shock, and the Indians will give way. Every man to his duty!"

The injunction to "stand firm the first shock," was frequently repeated by the officers. Colonel Butler ordered his men to fire, and at each discharge to advance a step. About four in the afternoon, the battle began.

For a while the advantage was with the patriots. Their steady fire told, and in the open ground, under the skilful generalship of Colonel Z. Butler, who was a Revolutionary officer, the British line was driven back in spite of all their officers could do to prevent it. The Indians in accordance with their invariable custom, were concealed in bushes, from which they poured in a galling flank fire. The patriots stood up nobly to their perilous work, but it was not long before the overwhelming number of the enemy developed itself. The Indians completely outflanked the left, and the wing was thrown into confusion. An order for this wing to wheel back so as to present their front to the enemy was mistaken for an order to retreat. The savages charging in a body at the critical moment, with their horrid yells, threw the whole left into utter confusion. Colonel Z. Butler, seeing the panic, threw himself recklessly between the lines. "Don't leave me, my children, and the victory is ours!"

Too late! Every captain that led a company into action was slain. Individually, the men fought like heroes, and it would require a volume to give the recorded instances of valour. A portion of the Indian flanking party got between the Connecticut line so as to cut off their retreat to Forty Fort, and the retreating army pressed toward the river. Monocacy Island offering the only hope of crossing, the stream of flight flowed in that direction through fields of grain.

The scene that now ensued baffles description. The tumultuous retreat to the river—the scores overtaken and tomahawked—the struggles in the water—the encounters on the island—the torture of the captured prisoners—the murders of that demon Queen Esther—the consternation of the settlers, and their flight through the wilderness—their sufferings—the carnival of death—all these have been described by a far abler pen than ours, and to that pen we must refer our readers.* It only remains for us to give a few episodes of the massacre of Wyoming.

CHAPTER III.

THE QUAKER PREACHER.

A SHORT distance from the main road leading out of Wyoming Valley, stood a residence somewhat superior to those in its immediate neighbourhood. Its construction and surroundings betokened an owner of both wealth and taste. The house itself was of a pure glistening white, which shone pleasantly through the luxuriant shade-trees by which it was enveloped. The garden and out-buildings all betrayed the hand of culture; and in short,

* Charles Miner, whose excellent history is an invaluable contribution to American literature.

it was one of those houses that arrest the traveller, and tempt him within its cool retreat and hospitable doors.

The house in question had been built by Major Abingdon, of the Continental Army. At the present time, he was so far removed, that it was impossible for him to reach the Valley in time to take part in the battle. His son, George, however, was one of the officers who resigned and hastened homeward to the protection of the loved ones who needed his assistance so sorely; and, at the moment we introduce the family to notice, he was marching out from Forty Fort with the column to attack the combined force of British and Indians. The painful anxiety of the family, who were sensible of the state of affairs, may therefore be well understood.

Mrs. Abingdon, a refined, intellectual lady, of some fifty years, was walking back and forth, on the covered porch that extended along the front of the house, her apprehension so keenly alive that it would not allow her to remain quiet. Annie, her daughter, whose face revealed the same delicate, intellectual beauty that was still traceable in the countenance of her mother, was standing on the steps that led down from the porch, looking off toward the settlement, which was impenetrably veiled by the intervening forest. Her cheeks, naturally rosy, were white, with the exception of a faint tinge in the centre, like that which is discerned on the face of the sea-shell, her blue eyes now round and full, and the attitude which she had taken, all conspired to lend an additional charm to her countenance and figure.

At the front gate, a rod or two away, stood Arthur, a boy not more than ten or eleven years of age. Young as he was, he was mature enough to understand that a fearful crisis was hanging over the valley that contained his beloved home, and child-like, he had gone to the utmost limit that parental authority would allow, in the hope of gaining the earliest tidings of the fortunes of the day.

"I scarcely dare hope," remarked the mother, as she paused beside her daughter. "I saw, when George went away, that he was not satisfied either with the appearance of things in the Valley."

"He could not help being anxious, mother, until the battle took place—his appearance was natural."

"There was too much of it. He was hopeful when he and the rest of the officers came home; but did you not observe how depressed he seemed after his return from Forty Fort?"

The daughter had noticed this, and she therefore evaded a direct reply.

"There are full three hundred men in the fort—a powerful body, it seems to me."

"Powerful enough, if they were only men, Annie; but remember there are feeble grandfathers, and boys scarcely larger than Arthur, and very few of them have ever been in battle before. If they had to confront British soldiers alone, I would not care the half that now distresses me; for, if defeated, they would be treated magnanimously by their conquerors. But those Indians, nothing will restrain them if they should gain the upper hand."

Annie felt the truth of what her mother had uttered, and her heart sunk within her. Besides her dear brother George in the battle, there was another exposed to danger, who was connected with her by tender and peculiar ties. Stoddard Franklin, a young Quaker preacher, who lived almost under the shadow of Forty Fort, had, for nearly a year, occupied the place in her heart which it is possible for only one human being to possess. There was a nobility about the man—a superiority of taste and intelligence, that raised him far above those surrounding him. A congeniality of feeling, and an appreciation of each other's excellence, had attracted the young people toward each other, until but a month or two previous they had exchanged vows, and mutually pledged themselves.

Young Franklin held a most peculiar position. He had no relative within hundreds of miles; but he was loved by those around him, who understood his sterling qualities, and he esteemed them in return. As each day and hour made it more manifest that war was to visit the Valley, his position became more trying and distressing. Had he not been an acknowledged leader of the Friends, one to whom they looked for example, guidance and direction, it is doubtful whether he would have hesitated a moment.

By principle a non-combatant, he had taken no part in the difficulty between the colonies and the mother country. More than once, he had been placed at the mercy of the Indians, but never was he offered harm, so well and widely known were his sentiments. In common with some of his neighbours, he had refrained from joining expeditions against the different tribes, and was looked upon by both parties as perfectly neutral.

But " grim-visaged war" assumed another form when the invasion of the settlement was threatened. As the impending clouds became darker and darker, and finally shot red lightning, and his numerous professed followers flew to arms, he began to act and feel far differently. It was observed by several of his acquaintances that, for a few days before hostilities commenced, he took his rifle and went alone into the woods. Ordinarily this would have attracted little attention, but one of them, from curiosity, followed him. He saw him penetrate the forest to a considerable distance, and then pause and look around him, as if to make sure he was not observed. Then, affixing a mark to a tree, he retired a hundred yards or so, and began practising upon it with his rifle. The Friend smiled, and mentally concluded that "Brother Franklin" would not be found wanting at the critical moment. Whether he was right or not in his conclusion, will soon be evident.

"But, mother, do you think they will gain the battle?" asked Annie, alluding to the last remark made by her parent. "You are usually so hopeful and confident, that it seems strange for me to attempt to console you."

"I do not need your consolation, Annie; you feel the alarm as much as I do. It may not be best to let Arthur know all, but there need be no concealment between us."

"You are right; I believe I have more terror this minute than you have experienced all day. I think there is scarcely a shadow of success for us."

"You have a double anxiety. You are alarmed for George and for Stoddard."

"I wonder whether he will fight," remarked the daughter, referring, of course, to the person last named.

"I have no doubt of it. If he does not, I shall never entertain the least respect for him."

Annie made no answer, for, in her heart, she entertained the opinion of her mother. She could defer to moral principle; but in a moment like the present, she could conceive of no conscience that would allow any human being to remain a passive spectator, when youth, beauty, innocence, and old age implored in vain for mercy.

"I am sure he will do all he can to defend the helpless. I know him well enough to say that with certainty," added the mother, who noticed the thoughtful look of her daughter.

"Yes; I am also certain he will. He is naturally chivalrous, and no woman or child can appeal to him in vain for protection."

"Nor man either, I trust——"

"Hark! hear the guns!" exclaimed the daughter.

"Yes; they are fighting. The battle must soon be decided."

"Oh! if we had a place where we could overlook it!"

The last observation was overheard by Arthur, who instantly said:——

"I know where I can see it! Up in the top of that tree!"

"But are you not afraid to climb it?"

"No, indeed," he answered, hurrying away. A moment later he was going up through the limbs with the agility of a monkey. When on the very topmost branch, he called out:——

"Oh, mother! I can see the whole valley and everything."

"Do you see the soldiers?"

"Yes, yes; our men are firing. There are the British soldiers, but not the Indians."

"They are hidden in the woods."

"Yes; I know where they are. I see smoke rising from the bushes. There must be somebody there to shoot the guns. Oh, mother and Annie! you ought to see the women and boys and girls."

" Where are they ? "

" They are standing off a-ways, looking on. If they all of them had guns I bet they could lick the Injins."

" How goes the battle ? "

" Oh ! they're fighting and fighting and fighting ever so hard. I can't see some of the men for the smoke. Now the smoke clears away. I see men down on the ground, and a good many others keep falling ! Oh ! I know what's the matter. They're getting shot ! "

The simple-hearted child did not reflect that perhaps his own cherished brother was among those stretched lifeless on the plain.

" I wonder whether Pete can be in the battle ? " exclaimed Annie, suddenly recollecting that their negro servant had not been seen since morning.

" Perhaps he is— "

" Oh, mother · mother ! can't you climb up here ? " called out Arthur, in great excitement.

" What is the matter now ? "

" There are hundreds and thousands of big Indians running out of the woods. Don't you hear them yell ? "

" And what are our soldiers doing ? "

" They're firing jolly—how they're pitching in ! By Jiminy ! it's no use ! they can't stand it ! "

" What do you mean ? What do you mean, Arthur ? "

" The men are running like all fury, and the Indians teaming after them ! You ought to see 'em trampling down the grain. Oh, mother, they're spoiling it all."

Mother and daughter looked at each other. Both understood that the carnival of blood had begun.

" What shall we do ? "

" We must leave ; they will be here."

" Where shall we go, mother ? "

" Almost anywhere, so that we get away from the Valley before the Indians come upon us."

" But will not the British officers restrain them ?"

" They cannot—no one can restrain them."

" But shall we not wait until George and Stoddard—"

" They may never come! Arthur, what do you see now ?"

" The Indians have got behind the men, so they can't get back into the fort, and they're all stretching it across the fields toward the river. But tain't no use, for the Indians are giving them fits. They can run a great deal the fastest."

For a half-hour more the boy remained in the tree, momentarily announcing the principal points in the panorama passing before his eyes. At the end of that time Mrs. Abingdon summoned him down, and ordered him to the stable, to bring forth two of their horses, for the purpose of taking the road towards Stroudsburg. The savages were already scattering through the settlements, and an hour more might be too late.

What few things they most needed were hastily gathered together and placed upon the horses—two noble animals—either one of which could have easily carried the three with their baggage. In accordance with her invariable custom, Mrs. Abingdon then secured the doors and shutters of the house, placing the key in her pocket, under the fond hope that she might soon return and find all undisturbed.

CHAPTER IV

A BLACKFOOT RACE.

"'Specs dere's goin' to be a mighty big fout to day!" soliloquized Pete Weldon, a large, overgrown negro, as black as the "quintessence of midnight," as he walked away from Major Abingdon's residence toward the wood. He was a servant who had been reared by the major, and who, from long association with the family, stood on rather favoured grounds—which, expressed in other words, means that he did very much as he pleased.

Pete was associated with an old man of German extraction who managed the farm, while the major and his son, the lieutenant, were absent in the army. Two or three days before, this man had followed the latter to Forty Fort, so that Pete was the only man left to assist and protect the females. The lieutenant gave the negro permission to join them if he so wished, but did not invite him to do so, as he was morally certain his presence would be of no benefit at all, to say the very least in the matter. Pete made answer that he would "'liberate'" upon the subject, and let them know what he had decided to do by the week following.

Taking a rusty musket that he occasionally used in hunting, he sauntered into the wood, on the forenoon of that memorable 3rd of July, decided upon only one thing—to keep away from the battle-field. The more effectually to accomplish this, he had concluded not to return to the house until nightfall, when he could not be urged with any reason to leave it.

"Yes, dere'll be a mighty big fout—dat may be set down as sartin; and de best t'ing dis coloured feller can do am to steer clear of all diffikilty, till dar' ain't no diffikilty to steer clear of, den dar' won't be any diffikilty. Dat's so, I 'specs."

He walked on a few rods and then resumed his musing :—

"I laid in a big stock ob food dis morning at breakfast, so dat I won't be hungry afore night. I'll jis' keep shady in de woods till de diffikilty blows over, and den I'll leave."

It did not seem to enter the African's mind that it was possible for his friends to encounter such a thing as defeat. It seemed to him that if any were invincible, they were the "Leftenant, and the old Dutchman," who had learned the art of war half a century before.

"I'd kinder like to see the fout go on. I nebber see'd one yet, and I s'pose it's high old fun. But dar' must be great danger in looking on. Dem Injins hate coloured folks, and I've heard dey could smell 'em a half-mile 'way. Mighty qu'ar!"

Pete by this time had reached a point almost back of the settlement. The day was warm, and he concluded to lie down on the leaves and sleep for a while. Like most of his race, he possessed a remarkable "gift of sleep," being able to pass off into unconsciousness at almost any time and in almost any place. Arranging a rude bed upon the leaves, he stretched himself beneath a large oak, and had scarcely done so when he was soundly asleep.

It was afternoon when he awoke—and the sound of musketry and the shouts of men aroused him to consciousness. He started up alarmed and bewildered, until he recalled his situation.

"De fout's begun," he exclaimed excitedly. "Oh! if I was only dar', wouldn't I smash t'ings!"

He took good care, however, not to be there, or any-

here that threatened danger. Rising to his feet, he ex-
mined the priming of his gun, brushed the leaves from
is person, and looked around to make sure that no
laring Indian's eye was fixed upon him.

"Best to be sart'in and ready—no telling when dem
ivages are 'round. Dey come frough de woods like a
it when she's going to catch a mouse."

As the firing increased in rapidity, and the terrific yells
f the assaulting Indians grew louder and louder, Pete
artook somewhat of the excitement, and his curiosity
ecame great to witness what was going on.

"I'll kinder stole up, and take a peep. It wouldn't
o for 'em to see me, as dey'd just as lief hit a feller when
ey shoot as not, so I'll keep shady awhile."

With this determination, the negro set out for the
cinity of the battle-field. He moved very stealthily,
ausing every few moments to look around him. Natur-
ly cowardly, his nerves were severely tried in thus
ealing up to a scene that from the very nature of things
ust be exceedingly dangerous. More than once he
alted, with that peculiarly wild and uncertain expres-
on upon his countenance—not knowing whether to go
urther, or to break and run at the top of his speed in an
pposite direction. The battle, which was becoming
ercer each moment, drew him on as the loadstone draws
e magnet—and at length he reached a point from
hich he gained a glimpse of the dreadful scene.

It required but a glimpse, indeed, to see how sadly the
ay had gone against the settlers. At the moment the
iew was opened to the negro, the rout was complete.

"I tells yer what, de white folks am catching it," he
oncluded. "I'm afeared these quarters are beginnin' to
it hot. Ki, yi! what dat man coming this way fur?"

The last exclamation was caused by the sight of a terrified man running headlong toward him. The suspense of Pete turned into alarm when he saw that the man was pursued by two Indians.

"Golly gracious!" he muttered, looking wildly about him. "S'pose that Injin sees me, what'll come of me?"

With that blind, wild feeling which takes possession of persons when seized with a panic, he turned and rushed frantically away, only seeking to get beyond sight of the terrible savages, who were already becoming furious from the sight of blood. He would have been successful had he exercised ordinary prudence; but a horse tearing through the undergrowth would not have made more of a racket than did he. The consequence was, that one of the Indians descried him, and, confident that his companion was all sufficient for the white man, he started in pursuit.

The consternation of Pete when he realized that a murderous Delaware, with upraised tomahawk, was seeking his life, can scarcely be described. He kept glancing behind him, and shouting at the top of his voice. As a natural consequence, he ran plump against a tree; but, as it was his head that struck, he suffered little injury.

The excessive terror of Pete gave him such fleetness, that for a few moments he really distanced the savage. He hoped that in the thick wood and undergrowth he might elude him altogether, but was not long in discovering that such was beyond the range of possibility. Scarcely conscious of what he was doing, he left the wood, and came into the open plain, where there was not the remotest chance of escaping the savage.

Pete did not join the regular stream of fugitives, else he would have assuredly fallen beneath the tomahawk of some vengeful red-skin. In his blind alarm, he crossed he road and tumbled over the fence into a wheat field. By this time, his pursuer was almost close enough to ring him down, but forbore, as there was every probability of making a certain thing of it.

The terror of the negro once more gave an extraordinary impetus to his speed, and he held his own until lose to the fence upon the opposite side of the field. As e was about to scramble over this, he descried a drunken oldier lying on the ground, with a jug beside him.

"Say, man, dar's an Injin chasin' me!" shouted Pete. "Shoot him, quick!"

"Three cheers for quick!" hiccupped the soldier, rising o the sitting position, and looking stupidly around him. What's up, to make you r-r-un so?"

"Dar's an Injin?"

"W-w-here might he be?"

"Right ahind me."

"All r-r-ight. I say it's all r-r-right; I'll drop him for ou."

Fearful of the inability of the soldier to save his own rown, Pete had paused but a moment to acquaint him vith the state of things. As the Indian came behind he soldier sitting upon the ground, he seemed to take in he situation at a glance, and to understand that he ould return and dispose of the soldier at his leisure, vhile the fugitive demanded his immediate attention. Accordingly, he cleared the fence at a bound, and with n exultant whoop, held his tomahawk aloof.

The soldier by this time had staggered to his feet, and ushed his gun between the fence-rails. Drawing back he hammer with his whole hand, he dropped upon one :nee, and gazed (so far as it was possible for him to ;aze,) across the field in the direction taken by his enemy.

"Can't see you," he stuttered, "but I k-k-nows yer s-s-somewhere out that way, so here goes." Saying which, he discharged his gun, and the savage dropped dead.* Providence himself had directed the ball.

Pete ran a long distance after his pursuer had fallen, unable to understand that all danger for the present was past. When he finally discovered that no one was following him, he paused, panting, exhausted, and quivering, so that he could scarcely stand.

"Dat's what I call a purty close race. Dat Injin had hard work to get away from me. I'd had him sure, if de soldier hadn't drapped him."

His flight had led him in a different direction from the river, so that he was unseen by any human eye, and, wearied and jaded as he was, he sunk down upon the ground to snatch a half-hour's rest.

"Dat yer's hard work ! Pity I didn't catch dat Injin, so dat I mout sculped him, and took him home, but he runned too fast for me, so I had to let him go."

Occasionally, he raised his head, and peered over the top of the wheat, but he was in no danger, and he did not leave the place until he was throughly recuperated.

"S'pect dey's wonderin' at home where I can be all dis time, so de best t'ing I can do is to go dar', and set dar hearts at rest. I kinder s'pects when I get home, I'll eat a big supper, and go to bed and sleep off de bad effects of dis day's trouble."

No time was lost in carrying out this prudent resolution. Making a long *détour*, so as to avoid all danger of encountering any roving enemies, he re-entered the wood, and took a direct line for home. The shades of night

---

* An incident similar occurred during the Wyoming massacre.

were gathering in the wood as he hurried along, and he, in his simple nature, experienced almost as much alarm from this alone as from the vindictive enemies who at that moment were wandering hither and thither, devastating, destroying, and slaying.

" 'Taint safe to be out arter dark," he muttered, almost running in his alarm. " Dar's ghostes and spooks in dese woods, and I doesn't care about meeting 'em."

Shortly after, he came in sight of the house. Its unnatural stillness startled him, and he walked on tiptoe to the rear, where he was in the habit of entering without being questioned. The door was locked. He came around to the front, and found this was also secured.

" Golly gracious ! what's de matter ? Don't 'pear to be anybody at home," he muttered, as he sought to peer in the windows. Discovering no light, he raised the heavy brass knocker, and let it fall. It sounded startlingly loud, and he gazed around, fearing that some one he wished not to see might be attracted hither.

There was no response from within, and he was debating with himself whether to attempt a forcible entrance, or to retire quietly to the barn, and spend there the night, when he was frightened almost out of his self-possession by discovering a tall figure slowly approaching from the wood. The person, while yet scarcely visible, halted, and appeared to be reconnoitring the house, as if uncertain whether to advance or not. Pete was riveted to the spot where he stood. He durst not stir, for fear of drawing attention to himself, and he was certain that if attention should be directed toward the porch, he could not avoid discovery.

The stranger remained stationary a moment or two, and then came stealthily forward. Pete was already meditating some desperate expedient, when, with feelings of the greatest joy, he recognised him as old Gersh Smithson.

———

CHAPTER V.

STRIKE FOR YOUR ALTARS AND YOUR SIRES!

THE events that we have taken upon ourself to record make it necessary that we should go back once more to that memorable 3rd of July, 1778.

When Colonel Z. Butler announced to his men that he and his officers had decided to march out of Forty Fort and attack the enemy, there were numbers who noticed the absence of Stoddard Franklin. This was observable from the fact that even the most sceptical had agreed, from his words and actions, that he would be on the ground when the real " tug of war " came.

" If he hopes to shelter himself by staying out of the fight, he will find himself mistaken," remarked one, who was rather envious of the good reputation the young man bore, and was therefore secretly pleased at the temporary cloud under which his name rested.

" I can't understand it," remarked a second. " We didn't expect him to pitch into every flurry that came up —but if he shirks out of the fight at such a time as this, some one had better advise him never to show himself in the valley again."

" I won't believe, you needn't tell me any such stuff," replied old Mr. Neville. " I saw him with his gun this morning. He didn't say anything, but I could see that them grey eyes of his meant mischief. Depend on't, you'll hear of him afore the battle's done with."

" This is one of the times when Quakers can't get out of shooting guns. If I should find him skulking I'd shoot him," added the first speaker, with a meaning shake of his head.

All of these remarks had been overheard by Lieutenant Abingdon, and they caused him inexpressible pain. He did not doubt for one moment that he should find his friend, young Franklin, upon the ground, and one of the leaders in the defence. But he was nowhere to be seen ! Could he stand unmoved when Annie Abingdon needed a protector ? Could his betrothed wife call in vain for succour, when he was given strong arms wherewith to defend her ? It was with a sad heart that young Abingdon answered these questions as the facts themselves seemed to answer them.

The troops marched out upon the plain, as has been described elsewhere, and the first platoon had received their orders to fire, when it was observed for the first time that Stoddard Franklin was among them. Where he came from, no one knew, as it was certain that until that moment he was absent. The inevitable conclusion was that he had gone to the battle-ground alone. There was little time, however, for speculation, as the contest had begun in dead earnest.

There are men who will laugh and jest when Death is stalking directly among them; and when the Americans began to fall under the withering fire of the concealed Indians, and the old men looked unusually solemn, and the boys turned pale with emotion, then it was that the "regular soldiers" began to exchange jokes with each other.

"There's the young Quaker !" exclaimed one. " He has come out to fight on his own account."

"See how carefully he takes aim ! He is as cool as if he was hunting squirrels. I'll warrant every shot tells."

c 2

" I say, Franklin ! " called out another.

The call was either unheard, or, if heard, unheeded, in the din of battle : the soldier repeated it in a louder voice.

" What does thee want ? " demanded the young Friend, turning a face toward him that was strikingly beautiful from the strange illumination thrown upon it by the light of battle.

" So you've made up your mind to fight, have you ?"

" I can scarcely hear thee ; speak louder," shouted Franklin, in the din of conflict, inclining his ear toward him, as he reloaded his gun.

" I say you've made up your mind to give up Quakerism, and turn in and fight with us."

" This jesting is unseemly, and I have no time to indulge in it," was the reproving reply, as the unerring rifle again came to his shoulder, and sent its deadly messenger among the horde of red-skins that were now developing themselves in astonishing numbers.

As the savages became engaged, it was noticed that every few moments a yell was uttered, which was caught up and repeated five separate times, from which it was concluded that there were six different bands of Indians engaged.

" Remain steady ! " shouted young Franklin, as he observed signs of wavering among a portion of the men. " We are doing good execution ; keep steady ; remember thy wives and children that are watching thee."

At this moment, a portion of the British line began falling back, and the militia, naturally enough, commenced pressing rather imprudently forward.

" Have a care," admonished the young man, who, unconsciously to himself, was coming to be looked upon as a leader. "Have a care! That bush is full of Indians, and they are hurting us sadly."

It was evident that he spoke the truth, for at every rifle-crack from the undergrowth a soldier was sure to come to the ground. An attempt was finally made to dislodge them; and at the moment one wing was wheeling into position, the whole troop of Indians poured from the wood in one of their furious charges, yelling and whooping like so many demons let loose from Pandemonium.

With what anxious hearts the officers watched their men under this charge! As it was a flank movement, and the attempt was made to bring the faces of the men toward the soldiers, the fatal misconstruction of the order was made, and the men began to break and fly. Colonel Z. Butler came thundering forward on his horse, shouting for them to halt and re-form, and young Franklin dashed among them.

"Stop, stop, my men! There is no order to retreat! If thee fly, thy wives and children will be left to the tomahawk. Stand steady, and the day is thine."

A portion of the men halted, but the majority were "struck" with panic, and none but a military genius could have arrested them. Individual instances are recorded of heroism, but truth compels us to admit the utter defeat and rout of the American column.

"See," said Westover to George Cooper, "our men are all retreating; shall we go?"

"I'll have one more shot first," was the reply. At that moment a ball struck a tree just by his head, and an Indian springing towards him with his spear, Cooper drew up his rifle and fired; the Indian sprung several feet from the ground and fell prostrate on his face.

"Come," said Westover.

"I'll load first," replied Cooper—and it is probable this coolness saved him, for the great body of the savages had dashed forward after the flying fugitives, and were far in their rear.

On the right, one of the officers said to Captain Hewitt: "The day is lost—see, the Indians are sixty rods in our rear; shall we retreat?"

"I'll be hanged if I do," was his answer. "Drummer, strike up!" cried he, and strove to rally his men. Every effort was vain. Thus he fought, and there he fell!*

In the white heat of the battle, Franklin and Lieutenant Abingdon encountered. Both stopped short and looked in each other's faces.

"You here?" asked the latter.

"Where else could I be at this moment?"

"I know—but you were not in the fort."

"I fired with the first platoon. My hands have slain more than one being to-day."

"And I hope they will slay many more before the set of the sun."

The two pressed hands and separated. There was no time for idling. There were too few—ah! too few, left to defend their homes.

By this time it was manifest to the young Friend that the day was hopelessly lost. The wildest confusion prevailed. The sharp crack of the rifle—the Indian yell—the imprecation—the vain prayer for mercy—the thud of the tomahawk—the hurrying to and fro—these were the sights and sounds that met his gaze on every side. He had stood cool and collected, but the Pandemonium

* Milner's History.

began to affect him, and the fever of excitement coursed through his blood.

"Verily, this is terrible—such as I have not looked upon before. Yonder is an ungodly heathen, dealing death around him, but he cannot be impervious to a bullet."

He brought his rifle to his shoulder, but at the very moment of pressing the trigger, a wild shot, whether from a friend or foe he never knew, struck the lock and injured it beyond repair.

"That is bad," he muttered, as he lowered and examined the weapon. "But it may do me good yet."

The brawny red-skin at whom the gun had been aimed was not more than ten yards distant, and most probably observed the act of hostility, for, with one of the whoops which it would seem are involuntary with his race, he bounded toward him with uplifted tomahawk. Taking but a step or two, he hurled the weapon with tremendous force and unerring aim straight at the skull of the young man. The keen eye and quick perception of the latter, however, warned him of the danger, and "ducking" his head with the quickness of lightning, he allowed the instrument to whiz harmlessly by.

"Now of a surety it becometh me to defend myself," was the mental conclusion of Franklin. "Ungodly heathen, prepare to meet thy Maker!"

On witnessing the failure of his attempt at murder, the savage drew his knife, and sprung forward with the intention of ending matters very summarily in a hand-to hand contest. Had the young Quaker been less agile and powerful, there could have been no hope for him; but, at the moment of uttering the admonition we have just recorded, he had clubbed his rifle, and the very instant the

shaven skull of the Indian came within re
stant the stock described a lightning-like swoop, and came
down with such irresistible fury, that the aborigine could
not have gone to the earth more suddenly had a bolt of
heaven struck him.

"Verily, thy days are numbered, and thou canst not
sin any more," remarked Franklin, glancing around to
see whether he was about to receive a charge from anyone
else.

He now observed that his personal danger was becoming more imminent each moment. His flying companions had left him almost alone, and unless he soon
freed himself from the net that was closing around him,
it would be impossible to do so. He noted that the
majority were making for the river, and more for the
purpose of defending the miserable fugitives, than for a
regard of his safety, he joined them.

In the wheat-field, he came up with old sturdy Ben-
jamin Belknap, who, cool and collected, was retreating in
comparatively a leisurely manner.

"It is a sad day," remarked the old man.

"A bitter day, indeed. It might not have been, had
our men maintained their composure, and stood their
ground."

"They were not used to such scenes, and I s'pose they
couldn't help the panic."

"I cannot agree with thee; I think they could. They
were admonished of the necessity by Colonel Butler, and
by their captains and lieutenants."

"I see your gun is injured," added the old man
glancing furtively around him, as he hurried along.

"It was struck by a ball, when in my hands."

"Take mine, I am so wearied that I cannot use it."

"Thee may need it—keep it thyself. I cannot keep a shot from striking me, if the Lord so wills, even if I held a loaded gun."

"Well, Stoddard, you see how they are falling around us. Are you willing to remain by and assist me?"

"That I will indeed gladly do, and defend thee to the last."

"I will help you all I can, although I fear I am about used up. In the old French war it wouldn't have knocked me up like this."

"'Tis sad that necessity compelled thee to come forth."

"I was glad to do it—glad to do it," was the hearty response. "I only hope—God receive my spirit!"

The poor old man fell dead, pierced by the bullet of some dusky foe. Stooping over him to make sure that life had really gone out, young Stoddard lifted the gun from his hands, and hurried on towards the river.

CHAPTER VI.

A SAD DAY'S WORK.

WHEN young Stoddard reached the river, he found it swarming with fugitives and pursuers. The former were making for Monocacy Island, and numbers had already reached it, and were hurrying over its surface in quest of some refuge from their implacable enemies. As he had delayed his flight, he thereby gained some advantages, and also some disadvantages. In the first place, he had more personal freedom to choose his method of escape, as the majority of the enemy were occupied in attending to those that had gone before, although there were still enough in his rear to necessitate promptness, expedition, and cunning. On the other hand, if he meditated ap-

proaching the island, there was the greater danger of discovery, from the fact that numbers of the savages had
already landed, and would be likely to descry any others
that approached.

The flying men and boys naturally poured into the
river directly abreast of Monocacy, and were thus carried
down stream, in some cases so much that they almost
missed it. The Quaker therefore ran up the bank, and
entered the water at such a point that he was certain of
striking the upper end of the island.

A forcible reminder of his situation was given in the
fact that the moment he entered the water a whoop behind announced that a savage had scented him, and was
noways disposed to yield his claim. Stoddard had flung
away his rifle, and provided himself with a knife. He
was an excellent swimmer, and entertained little fear of
his enemy, if they could meet on anything like equal
terms. For greater safety he placed the knife between
his teeth, and plunging into the current, struck boldly out
for the island.

His Indian admirer was not much behind, and struck
out as resolutely as himself.

The aborigines take to water as naturally as ducks,
and the one in question made his way through the current like a " thing of life." However much the American
Indian may excel in some specialty—such as running,
leaping, swimming, or endurance—the Caucasian race is
his superior, provided the latter has devoted the same attention to either or all of those attainments. As the red-
man's life is spent in a warfare that develops nothing but
endurance, celerity, cunning, and treachery, so he
naturally surpasses in those respects the white man,
whose life has been given to entirely opposite aims. It

happened, however, that our young Quaker friend had spent many a leisure hour in the river, and he now reaped his reward. Try as much as he might, the savage found it impossible to gain a foot upon him. While he whooped, shouted, and flung himself half-way out of the water, much in the same manner as a wounded porpoise, Franklin went through the current like some frightened fish, anxious only to escape its merciless pursuer.

It was while flying in this-manner, that it occurred to our hero that he was acting in rather a cowardly manner in fleeing from a single enemy. He reflected, further, that if he wished for safety when he reached the island, he must be rid of his pursuer before doing so. A moment's rapid deliberation determined him to turn round and en gage him at once. Having fully made up his mind to do this, no time was lost in carrying it out.

The exultant Indian suddenly checked his outcries when he saw the white man suddenly turn around, and with knife in his teeth make toward him. If the action of the Quaker was unexpected by the Indian, that of the Indian was unexpected by the Quaker; for without wait ing a moment, he turned and fled in the utmost terror Franklin pursued with all the swiftness he could summon but very soon made the discovery that it was impossible to overtake him. Their skill in swimming was equal.

Finding it was useless to follow, Franklin relinquished the pursuit, and leisurely continued his flight toward the island. There were savages all around him, and the ut most circumspection was necessary to avoid them; but by great good fortune, he found himself within a few yards of Monocacy, with the river bottom within reach and to all appearance unnoticed by any of the savage upon the island.

He lay in the water as low as possible, to avoid attracting attention, and was about to make his way to the eastern bank of the island, when, at the instant with the crack of a rifle came the zip of a bullet within a few inches of his face. Turning his head, he saw an Indian stretched upon the ground, his whole soul evidently absorbed in the work of putting an end to the young man's career.

This put a new face upon affairs, as the savage was lying at the very point where he intended to land. Observing the failure of his first shot, the Indian proceeded very coolly to reload his piece, constantly glancing in the meanwhile toward his visitor, to see that he did not take himself off, before he had finished his pleasant business with him.

"Verily, this is a reception that I did not count upon," was the mental conclusion of young Franklin, as he maintained a stationary position, uncertain what to do. If he remained where he was, it was manifest he would soon be shot, and if he attempted to land, he would thereby expose himself to greater danger, as the savage could watch him and thwart every attempt to land. The only course seemed to be a retrograde movement, and he was in the act of executing this piece of strategy, when he observed the rifle-stock again go to the shoulder of his vigilant enemy. Watching him with eagle-like scrutiny, he ducked his head at the very moment the trigger was pulled, and thereby effected another escape.

Providentially, at this moment, Franklin observed a piece of wood floating down-stream, which he immediately seized, and at once turned it into an effective shield, by placing it between himself and the hostile rifle. By not recklessly exposing himself, when he knew this to be loaded, he insured his own safety, as no gun was capable of sending a bullet entirely through the wood.

How long this aspect of affairs would have lasted it is impossible to tell. Darkness, which was now coming on, would have probably terminated it ere long, had not the attention of the savage been attracted to something that was occurring behind him. Franklin observed him turn his head as if some signal had been made to him, and then rise to his feet and hurry away.

The whole proceeding might be a ruse to lure the young Quaker to his own destruction, and for a while he so regarded it. He carefully scrutinized the shore, and on one occasion he either fancied he saw, or he really did see, the tufted crown and glowing eyeballs of the red-skin, as his head stealthily came up through the grass.

"Thy cunning and treachery will compare with that of the Evil One," muttered Franklin, still dallying in the water and hesitating to approach. From some cause or other, there was a renewal of shots and outcries upon the island, as if some minor conflict had commenced. Maintaining his position for a considerable time longer, our young friend concluded that the patience of his adversary must be exhausted, and he therefore allowed himself to drift down the current toward the island.

With considerable apprehension he approached the land, and when he really found himself upon the edge of the water, he still hesitated to emerge entirely. He waited but a few moments, however, when he boldly came forth and crept up the bank.

Reaching the top, he carefully peered over, but saw nothing of the Indian who had used him as a target. Reflecting that his absence might be temporary, he made all haste to leave the spot, which in that event could not be otherwise than exceedingly dangerous. He saw figures running hither and yon, in all directions, and he durst not rise to his feet. On his hands and knees he crept over to the eastern side, where he took refuge under a clump of bushes that hung directly over the stream.

Safely ensconced in these, the Quaker looked furtively out. For some distance along the stream was similar growth, and he did not doubt that many and many a fugitive had taken refuge among them. Looking furtively out, he saw a soldier approaching, whom he recognized as a former inhabitant of the Valley. He seemed to be searching for some one, and Franklin was meditating surrendering himself and claiming protection, when, to his surprise, the brother of the soldier came from the bushes scarcely a dozen feet away, and walked up to him and called him by name.

"Ah! so you are here," said the soldier, cocking his gun.

"Yes, brother John, and I surrender to you."

"No, you don't."

"I will be your slave all my lifetime; I will do anything for you —"

"All very well," said the soldier, raising his gun and shooting dead his own brother.*

Several Indians who witnessed this unnatural crime

* This dreadful crime was witnessed by several concealed fugitives, and John Pencil, the fratricide, at the close of the war, fled to Canada, not daring to encounter any of his former friends or relatives. In Canada, he was twice set upon by wolves, and twice rescued by Indians. The latter began to believe, however, that the hand of God was in the matter. "He too wicked—too wicked; Great Spirit angry; Indian no more help him." Shortly after, another lot of wolves got upon his trail, and his days were thus miserably ended in the Canadian woods, a prey to the ravenous animals.

shook their heads in displeasure. "Too wicked! too wicked!" The inhuman fratricide, however, heeded not their remarks, but passed steadily on in quest of more victims. Not until this moment did the heart of Stoddard turn sick at what he had seen. He had been shocked again and again and again, but he had now become somewhat accustomed to the carnival that was raging. Never in all his imaginings had he dreamed of such an unnatural crime as this. He was not filled with indignation nor fury toward John Pencil—a sort of horror, that, from its very excess, made him deathly sick, overcame him for a moment. He had seen a white man do what no Indian —and in fact what no barbarian—could be bought to perpetrate!

When our young friend had recovered himself in a measure, he turned his attention toward the savages, some of whom were close enough for their features to be distinguishable. The great wonder to him was that these men did not institute a thorough search of the bushes which offered such a tempting concealment to the wearied and terrified fugitives. Especially was this to be noted, when one had issued from them in plain sight only a few moments before.

The young Quaker could not believe that they would pass them by until he saw them turn their backs and walk toward another portion of the island. He then began to be more hopeful than he had been since landing.

By this time, it was quite dark, which was a God-send to the fugitives that were concealed in the fields on Monocacy, or who were fleeing terror-stricken with their families through the woods in the direction of Wind Gap or Stroudsburg.

Franklin had concluded to maintain his present position, if possible to do so, until night had fairly set in, when he meant to return to the mainland, and make his way to the home of the Abingdons, whom, he had good reason to fear, needed his assistance.

For the last fifteen or twenty minutes, a singular rippling in the water just below him had attracted his attention; and before leaving the spot, he determined to find the explanation for it. It could scarcely be an enemy, as there was no plausible reason for his concealing himself, while the probabilities were that it was a companion in distress.

" Friend," called out the Friend, " I fear thou art in sore trouble. Is it so?"

The rippling ceased, but there was no reply.

" Have no fear, as I seek no harm to thee."

Franklin heard some one coming through the water toward him. Not perfectly satisfied regarding matters, he held his knife ready for any assault. The next moment, he distinguished a form through the darkness.

"Can that be you, Stoddard?"

" Verily, I am glad to see thee, George," exclaimed our hero, as with heartfelt joy he grasped the hand of Lieutenant Abingdon.

CHAPTER VII.

THE TWO FRIENDS.

THE joy of the meeting between Stoddard Franklin and Lieutenant Abingdon may well be imagined. Each had good reason to fear the worst regarding the other, and the discovery of their mutual mistake was, in one sense, like the return to life of friends supposed to be dead. Each had rashly exposed himself in the battle yet both had escaped the lot of so many of their acquaintances.

"Indeed I did not dare to think thee alive," said Franklin, "when I knew thy courage so well."

"And what do you suppose I thought of you—when I left you right among the Indians, firing right and left."

"The good Lord above favoured me, and watched over my flight! Ah, George! do your battles show you such scenes as we have looked upon to day?"

"No; never have I been compelled to hide from the fury of an enemy before, for we are fighting a civilized people; but it is devils that are turned loose upon us."

"If thou callest the Indians by that name, what dost thou call John Pencil? You witnessed the deed, did you not?"

"His brother Henry had been whispering to me for the last half-hour before John came in sight. When he saw him, he said: 'As sure as I live, there's brother John. I'll give myself up to him, as he is pretty sure to discover me, and he will protect me from the Indians.' I concluded to stay where I was, until I was detected, or was compelled to flee. I do believe I nearly fainted, when I saw that dreadful tragedy! I cannot bear to think of it."

"I suppose, George, we ought now to go to thy home, and attend to the folks."

"Yes; I am very anxious regarding them, and there is no occasion for our lingering near the battle-ground."

"The day is gone, and the heathen are let loose in the Valley. To-morrow will be the dreadful day. The battle and massacre have occupied them until dusk, so that the general devastation of the settlement cannot take place until to-morrow."

"To-night, then, we must get mother, and Annie, and Arthur away, or it will be too late."

"To-night is the most favourable time. Fortunately, I have travelled the forest-path between here and Strouds-burg, so that we need not hesitate on account of the darkness."

"Let us go at once."

"I would advise a little delay. The night has not fairly settled, and we may be easily seen."

"You cannot comprehend my anxiety, Stoddard. I thought of nothing but them all through the battle."

"My apprehension is as great as thine. Am I not directly concerned?" he asked, with rather a quizzical expression. "Thy house stands away from the main settlement, and, although it may be exposed at other times, yet it is fortunate for us on the present occasion, as it is not likely to receive a visit before to-morrow."

"The probabilities are as you remark, but there can be no certainty regarding the matter. Bands of Indians may have been roaming in every direction for the last few hours."

"I cannot help agreeing with thee," replied Franklin, with a serious expression. "The most favourable supposition we can make still admits the great peril that hangs over their heads."

"Ay! the greatest of danger."

"Remain here, George, while I creep up the bank and look around."

"Be careful, for it seems to me that the red-skins are everywhere."

The young Quaker had as good reason as himself to understand the latter fact, and he was not rash or reckless. Reaching a point that commanded the island, he looked cautiously around. The darkness prevented a full view, but he saw several shadowy figures flitting to and fro, and had no difficulty in distinguishing several savages, and in one case two fugitives. The latter, who had reached the island previous, had all concealed themselves, or gone on over to the mainland, and continued their flight. Accordingly, those that he saw must be new arrivals.

On the lower end of the island a fire was kindled, around which figures occasionally moved. The upper portion seemed comparatively deserted. Returning to his companion Franklin announced this fact, adding :—

" It is now dark enough to make the attempt, and that which offers the most safety is the one that I took in coming here."

" Don't let us wait, for I am in misery so long as I know the folks are uncared for."

Our two friends might have risen to their feet and passed directly over to the opposite side of the island, but this incurred more risk than either was willing to encounter at this stage of the proceedings. It was, therefore, decided to remain in the river until they should pass the upper end, when, if the coast was clear, they could strike boldly out from the shore.

The young Quaker took the lead—making his way with a studied caution that struck his follower as altogether superfluous, but it was not long ere he was compelled to see its wise prudence. They had advanced somewhat over half the distance when a suppressed "'Sh " warned the lieutenant that something was wrong. His friend was crouching down as if to avoid observation, and he instantly imitated the example. His heart gave a quick throb the next moment, as he observed an Indian coming down the bank and peering into the bushes which concealed them both. His search was not very thorough, and he passed Franklin without suspecting his presence; but it chanced that he pulled the bushes apart at the very spot where the lieutenant was watching him with such breathlesss interest. As he did so, the latter drew back, but not until the eagle eye of the redskin had detected him. A gratified "Ugh!" announced the discovery as he stepped down to claim his prize.

Seeing that concealment was no longer possible, Lieutenant Abingdon arose to his feet, that he might possess the same advantage as his enemy, and drawing his knife awaited the onset. Nothing loth, the savage descended the bank, and with drawn knife warily approached him. At this point, when his eye gleamed with the light of exultation, something very much resembling a thunderbolt came in collision with the side of his head, and he turned several grotesquely original summersaults through the bushes.

" Most bloodthirsty heathen, go thy way in peace!"

The heathen went.

Upon feeling for his knife, with which to assist his friend, Stoddard Franklin was surprised to find it was lost, and that he possessed no weapon of any kind. Still he was not to be deterred from assisting his companion. With a cat-like tread he stole up behind, and dealt him the stunning blow that doubled him up in the bushes and sent a little prudence in his head; for, scrambling to his feet, he hurried away, doubtless labouring under the impression that Colonel Z. Butler had marshalled the remaining men of his column beneath that same line of bushes.

" This vicinity is no longer safe; let us hasten away," said Franklin, hurrying rather recklessly through the water.

" No doubt that fellow entertains the same opinion regarding it," replied the lieutenant, who could not be otherwise than highly pleased at the neat disposition his friend had made of the aborigine. The words of the Quaker were wise, and were instantly acted upon.

A few moments later the two stood upon the edge of the Monocacy, ready to push off for the shore which each had left but a comparatively short time before. The darkness by this time was so great as to shroud almost everything in gloom, and while this beyond question was to the advantage of our friends, it still rendered the greater care upon their part the more necessary, to avoid running into some danger from which it would be impossible to extricate themselves.

" Now," said Franklin, " thou must be fully sensible, George, of the dire need thy family has for us. Should one of us be taken, the other may still prove their protector; but if both fall, they may well fear for themselves.

" That is too true."

" Thou therefore must see how important it is that one of us at least should escape to them."

" Cannot both as well as one ? "

" I trust so ; but to guard against all contingencies, I have to propose this : Our presence on this island has become known to one of the heathen, and he, we have reason to fear, has communicated it to the others by this time. Their allies are on both shores, searching for victims. Thou seest how natural it would be for them to think we had fled to one of the banks after discovering our danger, and they may have communicated with them, so that preparations are made to entrap us."

" What is it you propose ? "

" That we wade up stream as far as possible, and that

thou remain there, while I make my way to the mainland to learn whether it be safe for us."

"You have already displayed so much wisdom in dealing with the red-skins that I feel like deferring to your
judgment. I must acknowledge that they are an enemy
with which I am not accustomed to fight."

"Nor myself, either," smiled the Friend. "If all is
well, I will whistle for thee to come."

"If there's danger?"

"I will return to thee, and we'll try another way.
Good-bye!"

Lieutenant Abingdon watched the head of the gallant
fighting Quaker until it disappeared in the darkness,
when he turned his thoughts to his own situation, and
patiently awaited the signal for him to cross over to the
mainland, and to the dear ones at home, that absorbed so
much of his thoughts.

During all this time, in which we have so minutely
narrated the experiences of a couple of our friends, it
must not be supposed that repose and quiet had settled
with the night upon the Valley. From every direction
came the explosive crack of the rifle, the whoop of the
wild Indian, the cry of the victim, while the beautiful
Susquehanna Valley was illuminated by the lurid conflagration of its buildings. From different points in the
woods could be discerned the glimmer of the camp-fires,
and around some of these were being enacted scenes which
we gladly leave to the pen of the historian.

Stoddard Franklin had been gone about twenty minutes,
when the young lieutenant heard the report of a gun
very near the spot where he supposed his friend must be.
This filled him with apprehension, which increased as
minute after minute passed by without bringing the

signal he was waiting to hear. Could it be that his comrade had fallen after all? Had he passed through so many dangers to become a victim, when on the threshhold of escape?

Sad and despairing, Abingdon returned an answer in the negative, when he caught a plashing in the current, and instantly discovered a head slowly approaching the upper portion of the island. Confident of its being his friend, he raised his head and shoulders above the water, and was about to call out, when something restrained him, and he sunk back again. It might be somebody else, and he concluded to await further developments before making his presence known.

When the man walked out upon the island, there was just light enough to reveal the figure of an Indian.

"Too hasty again," muttered the lieutenant. "I need the presence of Stoddard to protect me from my own foolishness. Hello! can it be?"

His exclamation was caused by the faint but distinct sound of a whistle. He did not wait for it to be repeated, although that was done a moment later, but plunged into the current at once, and struck out for the mainland. The shore was scarcely visible when he discerned the figure of his cherished friend standing out in full view, as if there were no foe within a hundred miles.

"Is it all right?" inquired the lieutenant, in an anxious whisper.

"Thou mayest land in safety; I see none of the heathen, although there were one or two in the vicinity when I first came here."

"I feared you were shot."

"Thee alludes to the gun that was discharged near here, a few moments ago."

" Yes."

" Some one fired it down the river bank, and then plunged into the stream. I could not see the result."

There was no time to be lost in conversation, and the two at once set out to reach the Abingdon mansion. This was at a considerable distance, and it required great care upon their part. The lawless Indians were wandering in every direction in quest of plunder and life, and they were frequently discovered in startling proximity. By making a long *détour*, however, after the manner of Pete, they reached the woods in safety, and shortly after came in sight of the clean white house, that each supposed contained for him the dearest objects on earth.

CHAPTER VIII.

WHITHER ?

" THANK heaven ! the house is undisturbed," was the fervent ejaculation of Lieutenant Abingdon, as he and Stoddard Franklin emerged from the woods and approached the dwelling.

" How still everything is !" remarked the latter. " It seems as if deserted."

" They have gone in and fastened the doors and shutters. Oh ! how rejoiced I am that they have been spared."

The impulsive young man was pressing eagerly forward, when his companion laid his hand upon his arm. He turned round rather impatiently.

" George, I like not this strange stillness. Let thee be cautious !"

" But they are frightened," returned the son, a dreadful fear taking possession of him.

" Wait, thee knowest not who may be in there—"

"See there !" interrupted the lieutenant, pointing to the shutter, beneath which the rays of some candle or light were thrown outward. "I know they are there," he excitedly continued. At the same moment he placed his hand upon the knocker and gave a resounding stroke. Instead of an instant response, the light was instantly extinguished, and they detected the hurried movement of some one within. Immediately after all was still.

"I like it not," said Franklin. "Thy folks are not in there. 'Tis some one else."

"Who can they be ? Not Indians, for they would never act in that manner."

"Step from the porch and conceal thyself."

The two whisked down and took their station beneath the concealing shadow of the oak which had supported young Arthur, while making his observations during the afternoon. Here they watched with painful anxiety for some clue to the identity of those within.

About ten minutes later, they heard one of the upper windows cautiously raised. The moon was quite bright, but the darkness of the background prevented them from making out who was at the casement. The proceeding, however, seemed to convince the Quaker that whoever the person might be, he was a white man, and he determined to hail him. Keeping his body concealed, he called out in a suppressed voice :—

"Who's there ? We are friends, and thee has no cause to fear."

A moment's silence followed, and then the head and shoulders of old Gershom were seen.

"If I ain't greatly mistook, that's you, Stoddard Franklin."

"It is, indeed," returned the young man, stepping forth to view, "and George Abingdon is with me."

"Where is mother and Annie?" demanded the latter, looking up to the window.

"They are—"

"Oh, my golly gracious! my head's broke!" exclaimed Pete Weldon, as the sash came down with a terrific whack upon his crown.

"Pete, do you know anything about them? Are they not in the house? Where have they gone?" asked George, not able to repress his impatience when he saw that the head of Smithson was withdrawn.

"I'll tole you in a minute, as soon as my head stops hurtin'—blame nigh knocked my brains out."

Some one was now heard at the lock of the door, and the next moment it was opened, and old Mr. Smithson stood before them.

"Come in! come in!" he exclaimed, as if fearful of being overheard. "I am so glad to see you alive."

"Where's mother? For heaven's sake, answer my question," demanded the lieutenant, becoming irritated at this repeated baffling.

"They are gone!"

"Where? where?"

"Left, I suppose, some time in the afternoon, when they found the battle had gone against us."

"Where, do you suppose?"

"Can't tell. I started Jerusha off toward Stroudsburg, and then came over here to help your folks away, and found they had already gone."

"Did I not see thee in the contest?"

"Yes; I was there, Stoddard, and did all I could, till I found it was going against us, and there was no use of trying any longer, and then I started to take care of Jerusha and the baby. When I came here, I found Pete, who was half scart to death."

"Doesn't he know anything about them?"

"Hasn't seen them since morning. He says he was in the fight, too, but I don't believe it."

"It is more likely that he hid himself somewhere until it was over."

While conversing, Smithson had busied himself with his flint and tinder, and soon had his candle re-lit and the door fastened. At this juncture the negro, Pete, made his appearance, scarcely able to repress his joy at seeing his young master alive and unhurt.

"Gorry gracious! isn't I glad to see ye, and war' ye in de battle?"

"Yes, Pete."

"And did yer see me dar?"

"No, and nobody else saw you there; so let us have no more of thy disgraceful falsehoods. Thou wert hid in the woods when the contest raged."

The servant saw it was useless to attempt to perpetrate deception upon the shrewd Quaker, so he wisely forbore it.

"I was asleep—dat's de truf."

The company, with the exception of the negro, had seated themselves, and were gathered close together.

"Pete," said the young lieutenant, "I want the truth from you, and nothing else. What time did you get here to-day!"

"It was jis' gettin' dark, and dat am no story."

"Don't you know anything of mother, or Annie, or Arthur? Haven't you seen or heard anything regarding them?"

" Noffin' at all, Massa George."

The latter now turned to Gershom :—

" What do you say about them ? "

" I think they've seen how things was goin', and they made up their minds to leave afore they's taken away."

" What do you think, Stoddard ? "

" There is reason in the words of Gershom. It may be that—most probably it is."

" Had the Indians taken them away, do you think they would have left the house and barn unburned ? "

" Hardly ; it seems they have not come upon this pleasant retreat, but they may come any moment."

" If it was a deliberate flight, either Annie or mother would have left some sign behind—something to guide me in searching for them. This is the sitting-room. I see nothing here. Have you noticed anything ? "

Gershom replied that nothing had attracted his attention, and at the suggestion of the young man, he searched by the light of the candle the lower portion of the house. It need scarcely be said that nothing was discovered.

" If they have fled of their own free will," remarked Franklin, upon his return, " they would have gone upon one of the horses."

" That's it !" exclaimed Lieutenant Abingdon, striking the table with his hand. " That will prove it !"

" Let Peter go to the barn and ascertain whether there be any of the horses gone."

" Please, Massa Stobbard, I doesn't—doesn't hardly t'ink dar' am any ob 'em gone—doesn't seem wuf while for me to go to all dat bodily trouble," returned the negro, in considerable trepidation.

" Peter, move, or I will move thee."

There was no mistaking the meaning of that soft, low

voice, and keen glance. Pete demurred no further, but quietly slipped out of the door, and departed.

" Do you think he can be trusted ? " questioned young Abingdon, as soon as the door was closed.

" If he attempts any falsehood or deception, I shall harm him."

" He is such a coward, that I doubt his entering the barn in the dark, when he thinks there is reason to believe there are Indians in the neighbourhood."

" He may go away altogether."

" Not he; he will cling to us, so long as there is the shadow of danger. He cannot bear to be out of our sight for a moment."

" Does thee know, George, that we are placing our own lives in imminent jeopardy ?"

" How ? "

" By remaining in this house. The heathen are prowling in every direction."

" I think they will hardly reach this place before the morning, for the reason that their hands are full in the Valley."

" Begging pardon," said Gershom, " I must say it's my opinion you're mistook. I dropped a redskin not more than a hundred rods from here, while the rest were running the settlers toward the river."

Smithson thereupon gave the particulars of the incident recorded in the first chapter. The narrative, as may be imagined, created quite a sensation upon the part of the listeners. Young Abingdon shook his head :—

" That looks ominous for mother and Annie."

" It was but one that Gershom saw, and he was pursuing a fugitive who led him in this direction. I have hopes that they got off in safety."

"So have I : but even if they did, where are they to-night ? In the broad woods, that are filled with terrified women and children. What will become of Annie and mother ?"

"If not pressed too sorely, they will reach Stroudsburg safely. I am strongly tempted to advise thee to press on in that route, that we may overtake them."

"If they are mounted, it doesn't seem to me we have much chance."

"They must travel slowly at night. It would have been fortunate, Gershom, had thy strong-minded wife accompanied them."

"Yes," assented the delighted old man, "she would be a prize for anybody ! I tell you, you can't scare her out these woods. She's what I call a genius—such as you don't meet every day.

"I am sorry that they should go alone."

"Who knows but what Jerusha may have found 'em !" added Smithson. "'Cording to my calculations, they didn't leave far apart. If anything, your folks must have gone first, for I came straight from my cabin here, and found 'em all gone."

"You saw no signs of Indians ?"

"Nothing at all."

"Nor anything that was left behind to catch our notice ?"

"I didn't see any such a thing, but that ain't saying there wasn't anything about, 'cause I didn't think to look. There might have been lots of 'em."

"It was too dark for us to note any such thing when we arrived. It will not do to wait until morning, and there may be something of vital importance to us."

"I cannot see how it can be avoided."

" Would it not do—

" Hist !" interrupted Franklin, raising his hand. " I hear a cry from some one."

All paused, and while they were intently listening, there came the frenzied voice of Pete : "Injins ! Injins! Injins ! Dey's arter me ! Help ! help !"

CHAPTER IX.

TWO DISCOVERIES.

THE three men, with throbbing hearts, awaited more definite intelligence from Pete. Still rung his voice :—

" Injins ! Injins ! Help ! help !"

It should be remarked here that there were but two rifles in the company, one of which belonged to Smithson, while the other was the property of young Abingdon, he having recovered it after entering the house. The Quaker possessed only those arms which nature had furnished gratuitously. The three men had arisen to their feet, and with bated breath were listening.

" Likely he is frightened at some animal," said Franklin. " I can hardly think the Indians would act in that manner."

" They may—there he comes !"

At that instant the elephantine-like tread of Pete was heard, and he dashed into the house in wild terror.

" Injins ! Injins !" he shouted. " I seen seventy-five thousand of 'em, all settin' on de gate !"

" Be still, Peter, or I shall make thee !"

The servant quieted at once under the admonitory glance of Franklin, while the latter strode to the door and peered cautiously out. In every direction he looked, but saw no sign of a living person. He waited several

minutes but heard no sound. Satisfied now of the mistake of the negro, he came in with considerable righteous
indignation.

"Peter, thou art telling grievous falsehoods. I now
ask the truth of thee."

At the moment of asking the truth, he grasped the
negro by his collar and turned his face towards his own.
Peter stood in wholesome fear of the young Quaker, who
never said anything that he did not mean, and he made
no attempt to prevaricate.

"I see'd 'em—yes, I did, now,"

"How many?"

"Didn't count."

"How many does thee think?"

"ONE!"

"And where was he?"

"Layin' down ahind de barn-yard fence."

"Did he chase thee?"

"No; but he's jus' gettin' ready to—fac'—when I cut
grabbel for de house."

"Did he say anything?"

"Kinder groaned—didn't wait to hear any t'ing more,
'cause, t'inks I, it's gettin' mighty dangerous yerabouts,
so I cleared.

"Did thee look back and see him?"

"Yas;—sure that. Looked back and see'd him
climbin' ober ob de fence. T'ink he was afeard to foller
me in de house, 'cause he knowed Massa Franklin war'
about."

This diplomatic piece of flattery did not satisfy the
person against whom it was levelled of the extreme
danger that Pete had run. It more than convinced him
of his childish cowardice.

" You did not enter the barn, then ?"

" Golly gracious, no—guess not."

" What I thought," said the Quaker, turning toward Abingdon. "Tarry thou here, until I satisfy myself."

Instead of emerging from the front door, Franklin, after considerable manœuvring, let himself out of the kitchen, which being draped in shadow, afforded him greater safety in case the house was under surveillance. Fairly outside of the building, he controlled his movements by the greatest circumspection. While he did not believe that Pete had obtained even a glimpse of a hostile savage, he yet knew there might be many lurking in the shadow of the woods, and a thoughtless exposure might be followed by the sharp crash of the rifle and the unerring bullet.

While stealing along the fence, and when about a rod from the gate that opened into the barn-yard, the Quaker heard a noise as if made by a person crawling upon the ground. He paused, and looking in the direction indicated, discovered a dark figure in the act of rising. One penetrating glance showed that it was a large hog that was simply changing its position.

" Verily, Pete is a coward, to be so terrified at a harmless quadruped."

This discovery gave Franklin greater confidence, and he advanced toward the stable. It required but a moment to see that the two horses were gone ! Greatly rejoiced at this discovery, he set out to communicate as much to young Abingdon.

He was walking quite rapidly toward the house, when he stepped upon something that yielded to his foot. Stooping to examine it, he was astonished to find it an Indian moccasin. He held it up in the moonlight and

D

scrutinised it. This gave a new turn to his thoughts. The most natural inquiry was as to how it came there. And the most natural and only answer that presented itself was, that it had been dropped during the day by the owner—in fact, it was morally impossible that it should have lain there more than several hours at the most.

Dejected and thoughtful, Franklin began searching the ground for other evidences of the late presence of the Indians. The light was too obscure for him to detect those faint signs that could not have escaped his eye during the day-time, and he entered the house where young Abingdon was anxiously awaiting him.

" The horses are gone ! " was the answer to the inquiring look.

" They have fled, thank heaven ! "

" Hold ! I fear the worst ! "

" What have you discovered ? Do not keep me waiting."

Franklin walked into the room, and produced the significant moccasin.

" I found that lying in the yard. Does it not tell its own story ? "

Old Gershom took the article and examined it.

" A genuine one, that's sartin, and it isn't three hours since it was on the foot of a redskin."

" But why should he leave it ? "

" He has not cared for it. The weather is warm, and I s'pose likely as not he's throwed it away, preferring to go barefoot. Maybe the other one isn't fur off."

" They have been captured, I fear," said Franklin, after a moment's silence.

" But the horses ? "

" Have been stolen. Perhaps they have been allowed

to ride away. Could we know their direction, we might reach them before the morning sun."

" Is there no way of determining it ? "

" I s'pose yer might send one ob us on to de Injins, and ax 'em which way dey am trabeling," was the lucid suggestion of Pete.

" Would thou be willing to perform that duty ? "

" Mi'ty willin', but jis' now 'fer to be 'scused. Didn't see nuttin', Massa Stoddard, ob de savages 'round de barn?"

" Neither thou nor I saw any."

" Shall I tell you whar' dat moc'sin come from ? "

" Do you know anything about it ? " asked Lieutenant Abingdon, in all seriousness.

" Doesn't know for sartin, but I t'inks de old feller dat chased me dropped it. I kinder heard him slip, and to my mind dar' ain't no doubt but what he am de genuine owner, and I s'pectfully s'gests dat you 'turn it to him, to keep his good will."

George in disgust turned to his friends.

" What is your opinion, Gersh ? "

" I think Stoddard is right. All three have been taken away by the Indians themselves."

" Then we are losing precious time by sitting here in idleness."

" I do not see how it can be well avoided. We are powerless to help them so long as night lasts, unless Providence should guide us."

" Let us all go out and search the yard. We may stumble upon something that will give us a clue to their fate."

" As we are incurring great danger by remaining in the house, when the heathen are raging all around us, we can do nothing less than change our quarters."

All went out of doors. Stoddard Franklin would have made a consummate backwoodsman or a frontier scout, for they had scarcely emerged into the yard, when he took in the situation with a hunter's eye. He felt there was danger of the Indians coming upon them unawares, and he saw at once that the most probable point at which they would appear was toward the settlement.

" I will keep a look-out while ye continue the search, unless the heathen see us before we see them."

He hurried across the yard, and went a hundred yards or so away, in a spot where he could conceal his body and still have a view of the much-feared point, and of his friends who were ahead, examining the ground with all the minuteness possible in the moonlight.

The scene that met the eye of the young Friend was solemn and impressive. In different directions the glare of burning buildings was thrown against the sky, and the shouts of men came upon the air with fearful distinctness. Never until that day had he mingled in any scene of violence or bloodshed. He had stricken down and slain several fellow-creatures. Ay! he who was looked upon as the champion of those who would tolerate war upon no terms—he had mingled freely in the fearful contest, and eagerly slain the enemies around him. But he felt no reproaches of conscience. On the contrary, he never heard more unmistakeably its approving voice.

The meditation of the young Friend did not prevent his maintaining a vigilant watch. He could discern his companions groping in the yard, while all around was perfectly still. The dark woods, that came up in one portion within a hundred yards of the barn, were as silent as if they contained no living thing—a treacherous silence that boded no good to those in waiting.

Left entirely alone, Stoddard Franklin fell to speculating upon the fate of the fugitives. The thought that they were slain could not be tolerated—the conclusion that they were captured was inevitable. There was no doubt at all in his mind regarding this. Until the moccasin had been discovered in the yard, he had hoped, with good reason, that they had taken the alarm in time, departed upon their horses, and made good progress toward Stroudsburg.

The thoughts of the young man naturally turned toward Annie, whose fate so greatly concerned him. Was she looking for rescue through his assistance? Did she believe he had taken so active a part in the contest of the day? Did she believe (and this supposition caused him more pain than anything else), that he would avoid the conflict, when every arm in the Valley was so sorely needed?

He was in the midst of these reveries, when his ear caught the snapping of a twig. His first proceeding was to step behind a tree, so that his body was sheltered against any demonstration from the quarter where danger was thus announced. A low, quavering whistle announced to Lieutenant Abingdon and old Gershom the state of affairs, while the Quaker turned his eagle-eye towards the suspicious point.

He had not waited five minutes, when he distinctly made out the form of a person moving forward on the ground. Had he possessed a rifle, he would have doubtlessly discharged it, and thus disposed of the difficulty in the most summary manner. But he had no gun, and could therefore only watch and wait.

Nearer and nearer crept the dark body, until but a small space intervened between the two. The sentinel could follow every motion without difficulty, and he noted that he was coming straight toward him. This convinced him that either the Indian was attempting to steal upon him unawares, or he was not conscious of his presence, and of the fact that his every motion was observed.

"Hallo! Stoddard, that you?" came an inquiring voice. The person speaking arose to his feet, while Franklin stepped toward him, recognizing as he did so, the voice and figure of young Arthur Abingdon. The next moment, he was led toward the house, where his story was soon told.

CHAPTER X.

THE CAPTIVES.

ANNIE ABINGDON had mounted her horse, and her mother was in the act of mounting, preparatory to flight, when footsteps caught their ear, and turning their startled gaze, they saw two hideously-painted Indians, all grimy, scowling, and baleful, come around the corner of the house, and rapidly approach them with their peculiar sidling trot. The fugitives had good cause for apprehension at sight of their inhuman captors. Tales of horror had reached their ears of the outrages of the red men, and they might well be terrified at their approach. But there seemed no avenue of escape. Each of them held a rifle in his hand, and in case of attempt at flight upon their part, there was no doubt but both would be used.

"Shall we not fly?" whispered Annie, adjusting herself on the horse, and ready to give him the rein.

"No, we shall both be shot."

"And tomahawked if we remain."

"Too late now to help ourselves."

Arthur seemed to entertain a different opinion, however; for, finding the Indians were bent on securing them, he shouted :—

"Don't you come nigh me, or you'll get your heads smashed," and thereupon started to flee.

"Mother, stop him!" whispered Annie, "or they will shoot him."

"Arthur! Arthur! come back instantly!" called the parent.

Thus appealed to, the boy paused, as if undecided what to do. A repetition of the command brought him reluctantly back. It was well he obeyed, for one of the savages had already raised the hammer of his rifle, preparatory to putting a most effectual check to his flight.

"Are you not ashamed to go and leave your mother and sister when they are in trouble?" asked Mrs. Abingdon.

"I didn't think about that," replied the lad, hanging down his head, "but I thought as I couldn't do you any good by staying, I might as well run off and hunt up George and Stoddard, and see if they couldn't put a stop to this."

"I wish you could have done so," said the mother, in a low tone, "but they would have killed you."

"Never mind, mother, I'll give 'em the slip afore long," whispered the boy.

At this moment, one of the Indians caught the bridle-rein.

"Ugh! no run! tomahawk! kill!"

The mother was on the ground, but Annie had mounted the horse. Not suspecting any personal indiguity, she was unprepared for the insult of the Indian, who, catching one of hands, jerked her to the ground.

"Stay dere.   Hoss be ours!"

The girl's eyes flashed fire, and her cheeks burned with indignation.   She looked at her insulter as if she would have annihilated him, had the power been hers; but he seemed stoically indifferent to her actions.   Understanding that the captives were too thoroughly frightened to attempt escape, the two Indians drew to one side, and began consulting together.   Their looks and gesticulations showed that they were conversing in regard to the barn and house; and the ladies needed no other evidence that the question under consideration was, whether they should be destroyed by fire or not.   The one who had seized the bridle-rein appeared to be strongly in favour of it, and gesticulated and shook his head as if out of patience with the restraint imposed upon him.   His companion seemed to be reasoning with him, and interposing some strong objection.   This state of affairs was so palpable to the captives, who were huddled together, furtively watching their enemies, that they adopted a rather clever ruse to save their dwelling.

"They mean to burn it," said the mother, alluding to the project that then occupied the mind of every one, with perhaps the exception of her son.   "They mean to burn it.   See how they keep pointing to it, and making all manner of gesticulations."

"It is only one of them—he who pulled me off the horse.   The other doesn't want him to wait."

"It won't take much to persuade him, I fear."

"Oh, mother! must this house be burned to the earth, and we made homeless?" wailed Annie, the tears coming to her eyes.

" I am afraid there is no help for it. It all depends upon the disposition of that one who now seems opposed to it."

For several moments, mother and daughter stood clasping the boy between them, and watching in terror their captors, when Annie suddenly spoke in an excited whisper :—

" I know what the trouble is, mother. I know why one of them doesn't want the house set on fire."

" How should you know, my child ? "

" It is pretty near night, and they are afraid the light would be seen by some one who would pursue them, before they could get far enough away with us."

" If George or Stoddard would only come."

" Let us make believe we expect them."

" How can we do that, my dear child ? "

" I will show you."

Drawing a white handkerchief from her dress, she held it aloft and waved it, as if signalling to some person in the distance. Taking the cue, young Arthur shouted, " Yes, hurry up, George."

Both the Indians turned as quick as lightning, and he who had seemed so anxious to burn the buildings strode forward, with his hand laid threateningly upon his knife.

" Stop ! stop, Annie ! " whispered the mother. " See how angry he is ! "

" Put down ! kill ! stop dat ! " admonished the savage, stepping directly in front of her, his eye gleaming, and his brow as black as a thunder-cloud.

" Kill me, if you dare ! " exclaimed the girl, her eyes flashing defiance and scorn. " You are not fit to live, and I am not afraid of you."

And then she deliberately rose on tiptoe and waved her

handkerchief again, giving the redskin, at the same time, one of her glances that (ought to have) tumbled him over as summarily as a blow from the arm of the young fighting Quaker. The consequences of this daring act might have been serious, had not Mrs. Abingdon caught the arm of her daughter.

"Annie, I am displeased with you. Do not repeat such actions."

"I will stop for you, but not for him. I wouldn't obey him if he held his knife over my head."

The Indian, comprehending the true situation of affairs, now rejoined his comrade, who had not stirred a step during the occurrence, and they instantly began a conversation more animated than before.

The ruse of Annie Abingdon effected at least the object which it was intended to accomplish. It made both their captors believe that succour was too close at hand to admit of further delay. Accordingly, they both hurried back to where the ladies were anxiously watching their movements, and ordered them to mount one of the horses. Annie indignantly demanded to know whether they could not be allowed to have one apiece. The savage would hear of no parley, and commanded them to mount at once or else follow afoot. The daughter saw the entreating look of her mother, and, in addition, the flurry of her own feelings had somewhat subsided, and she had thus gained some prudence, which otherwise would not have been hers. She therefore obeyed at once, and just as the sun was setting, the party entered the woods, one of the Indians leading the horse by the rein, Arthur walking directly behind the animal, while the other Indian brought up the rear.

The course of this little party was through a sort of

bridle-path that for a number of miles ran almost in a direct line towards Stroudsburg. This made it extremely probable that they would fall in with some of the fugitives, who were beginning to scatter in every direction through the woods, although the majority were likely to take the Old Warrior Path, and the main routes to Stroudsburg and Wind Gap.

Had Mrs. Abingdon and her daughter been given a glimpse of what was going on at that moment all around them, they would have been thankful for the consideration with which they were treated. They could not tell where they were going, it is true; but they had little fears for their safety. They did not understand the depravity of the human heart. Their anxiety was regarding George Abingdon and Stoddard Franklin. Were either or both alive? Had they not fallen in the dreadful conflict?"

"If they were alive and knew," said the mother, as she held her daughter clasped to her heart, "it would not be long that we had to suffer this indignity.

"I fear for them, and yet I feel hopeful that they have escaped."

"You speak as though both were in the battle."

"Both were; I know it," returned Annie, confidently.

"How I have prayed and prayed this afternoon. Never did I plead with my Maker as I did to-day. And you?"

"Do you think I could have forgotten the only One to whom we could look? Ah! no, mother!"

"I am almost despairing. If poor George is killed, what will become of us?"

"I hope he is not; I seem to feel it. You are unusually low-spirited. Cheer up, dear mother."

"The woods are so gloomy that I cannot feel otherwise than deeply sad. The battle went against us, and who can tell what the dreadful consequences must be?"

"We are safe ourselves, which is more than many others can say."

"How can you say we are safe, when we are in the hands of these savages, who would as lief kill us as allow us to live."

"I do not think they would harm us—they seem to be well enough disposed toward us."

"How can you judge of their intentions ?"

"I cannot with certainty. I think they simply wish to make us prisoners, in the hope, perhaps, of getting a large ransom."

"It may be that, and it may be worse. We cannot surely call it safe to be placed in their power."

"I am certain I should rather be here than in our house to-night or even to-morrow. The most terrible time is to come. We have just escaped it."

"You feel more hopeful than I can. I wonder how Arthur stands it ? Arthur !" called the mother, looking around in the darkness."

"I am here, mother, but I don't expect to be here long."

"What do you mean ?"

"You just keep shady and I'll give 'em the slip, and go back to the house, and wait for George and Stoddard."

"Hush ! they will hear you."

"Let 'em hear ; they hain't got brains enough to understand what I'm saying."

"Can you find the way back ?"

"I'll bet I can ; I've been further than this in the woods before to-day—or to-night, I s'pose I now ought to say."

" Don't be rash, for if they think you want to get away they might harm you."

" I'd like too see 'em try it. They wouldn't want to do it again," said Arthur, with childish confidence. " How do you feel, mother and Annie ?"

" Very well; keep up a brave heart."

Mother and daughter now resumed conversation in a low tone. They had been engaged thus but a few moments when an exclamation from the savage in the rear attracted their attention. The one leading the horse instantly stopped and exchanged a few rapid sentences with his comrade.

" Arthur has gone," whispered Annie, " that is what the trouble is about. Just speak and see."

The mother called her son's name several times, but there was no response. He had kept his word, and slipped away in the darkness. As may be imagined, Mrs. Abingdon and Annie were gratified at this. In case George or Stoddard were living, it improved, in fact made certain, an attempt at rescue. And what could an attempt result in but success !

The Indians conversed together a few moments, and then appeared to give up trying to recapture the boy. The agile little fellow had gone beyond all hope of recovery.

The night was now considerably advanced, and the captors began their preparations for encamping until morning.

CHAPTER XI.

THE CAMP-FIRE.

MRS. ABINGDON and Annie were fortunate in being the captives of two Indians who treated them with such leniency. It was the fate of no other prisoners, and is accounted for by the fact that they belonged to a tribe in the South, who had joined the expedition chiefly for the sake of plunder. It was their intention to retain these valuable prisoners, confident that they would be claimed and ransomed by their friends.

The horse, after being stopped by the leading savage, was allowed to remain in the path, while one of the captors turned aside to find tufts and leaves wherewith to start a fire. This required but a short time, when a cheerful, crackling blaze ascended against the trunk of a giant oak. The ladies were now compelled to dismount and follow them to the spot, while the horse was secured to a small sapling.

" I wonder whether they intend to offer us supper," remarked Annie, who by this time had come to look upon her captors with very little fear.

" I doubt whether they have any to offer. I see nothing, at least. Do you feel hungry ?"

" No ; I could not swallow a mouthful."

" Nor could I, so we shall not be troubled regarding that. I suppose they intend remaining here all night."

" Mother, is it not strange that they should do it, when they know Arthur has gone, and may bring pursuers ?"

" Yes ; it seems reckless upon their part. There are but two of them, and I think either George or Stoddard could come upon them stealthily and overcome them."

" By shooting one and rushing upon the other. I only

hope they will not stir from here before morning. I feel very hopeful now since Arthur has escaped. He deserves credit for it."

" Yes ; I can't understand how he accomplished it, with that one walking directly behind him."

" We must avoid showing any hopefulness or expectation of help, or they may move again. You know it was that which started us so soon this afternoon."

During this conversation, the ladies had stood side by side, so far from the flame that their faces and forms were only occasionally visible. No attempt at flight or escape upon their part could succeed, and indeed none was contemplated. The eagle eyes of the Indians, though seeming to take no note of them or their movements, never allowed them to be fully out of sight for a moment.

When the fire was fully ablaze, and enough branches had been collected to keep it bright for several hours, one of the savages spread his blanket on the ground, and signed for the ladies to take it.

" Shall we accept it ?" asked Annie, who could not avoid smiling at the grotesque politeness of the red man.

" Yes ; he may be offended if we refuse, and there is no occasion to make him feel ill toward us."

" He feels ill enough already, for that matter," said Annie, coming forward and taking her seat upon the blanket. The mother joined her, and the two men seemed rather gratified at the docility and good nature exhibited by their fair captives.

" Now," said the daughter, " we have rather a difficult part to play. We must be obedient and cheerful, and yet act as though we had no hope save in the clemency of these knights of the wood."

" You seem to have changed your disposition since

leaving home," smiled Mrs. Abingdon. "You were then fiery enough to brave his fury on a very trivial matter."

"He insulted me, and let him do anything like that again," replied Annie, the snap coming back into her dark eyes. "I am not afraid of them, and if I didn't feel almost certain there would be someone along this way before morning, I think they would hardly find me so tractable."

"It is best to remain so, dear child, whether our friends come or not. The savages are always better disposed toward the prisoners who do not occasion them trouble."

"If Arthur has the prudence to keep out of danger, I look upon it as almost certain that he will bring some one back with him."

"He is young, but he has learned a great deal since morning. Other enemies must be abroad to-night, and he may encounter them, but I do not think there is much danger."

"We must not forget to pray for him, for he is only a mere lad, and does run great risk. I place my hopes in this fact," said Annie, after a moment's thought. "He will go straight back to the house, and if George and Stoddard have escaped, or if anyone else feels any anxiety regarding us, they will most certainly come directly there."

"See! what is the matter now?"

The two Indians, who were seated by the fire indulging their pipes, both raised their heads as if something had attracted their attention. The two captives also listening, a perfect silence ensued; but neither of them could hear the faintest sound.

"Something is wrong!" whispered Mrs. Abingdon.

" Maybe something is right !" replied Annie, her heart beating high with expectation.

One of the savages at this point arose to his feet and stealthily disappeared in the darkness, while the other as cautiously drew back from the circle of light thrown out by the fire.

" I do believe some one is coming," repeated Annie.

" I pray God that it may be George and Stoddard."

" 'Sh ! don't you hear the sound of a horse's feet in the path ? "

" Oh ! it cannot be they, for they would not come on horseback."

" Some poor fugitives, running right into danger without knowing it. What a pity we cannot warn them."

The regular tramp of a horse walking along could now be heard, and, as well may be imagined, the mother and daughter waited with the most acute apprehension. They were in this nervous state of excitement, when both were startled by the shrill voice of a female :—

" Let go that horse, you black, nasty Indian, or you'll be sorry ! "

They recognised the tones, and looked at each other in amused dismay.

" Mrs. Smithson !" they gasped, simultaneously.

" What can she be doing here ? " asked the mother.

" Probably fleeing like ourselves."

" But where's Gershom ? "

" Maybe dead—"

Annie hesitated, fearful of uttering her thoughts. The failure of George and Stoddard to appear had filled her with a more terrible dread than she had experienced since the commencement of her captivity. The mother understood what she meant ; but further interchange of feeling was prevented by the scene so close by, which was rapidly becoming lively and interesting. The words of the Indians as usual were guttural and sententious, while those of Mrs. Smithson rung out sharp and shrill as a miniature steam-whistle.

"I tell you, let go that horse, or you'll wish you'd never seen me?"

As for that matter, the two savages had not yet fairly had a sight of the strong-minded woman. However, they did not seem to heed the direful threat, and persistently disputed her passage.

"I've got a bag of meal here, and if you don't want to get whacked over the head harder than you was ever whacked in your life, let go of that, right straight away."

A moment's silence followed, as if Mrs. Smithson had concluded to give them time fully to digest what she had uttered.

The next sound was a dull thump, such as would be naturally made by a person being struck with a bag of meal. Mrs. Smithson had kept her word.

"There! I told you I'd do it. Now, clear out!"

The next moment our friends heard the crashing of branches, and one of the Indians appeared, leading the horse, while his comrade walked in the rear, as if to prevent any attempt at escape upon the part of their new captive.

The surprise of Mrs. Smithson was great upon seeing Mrs. Abingdon and Annie quietly seated near the fire and gazing toward her.

"Why, how under the sun came you here?" she asked, totally oblivious of the presence of her captors. These were pointed to by Annie, as a significant answer.

"I understand," replied the woman, with a knowing

shake of her head. " Did you ever see such imperence ?—
stopping me, when I was going along, minding my own
business."

" They care nothing for our rights—else you would not
see us here."

" What they goin' to do with you ?" asked Mrs. Smithson, in her abrupt, impulsive manner.

" We cannot tell."

" I know they won't do much with me ? I ain't afeard
of 'em. If there wasn't more'n one, I'd make him
dance; but there's two—besides that, I've got this baby
to 'tend to."

" How came you here, Jerusha ?"

" Going to Stroudsburg."

" Is this the direct route ?"

" Good as any—the horse got out of the way 'fore I
knowed it."

" Why are you going to Stroudsburg ?"

" Because the plagued—hain't you seen Gersh ?" suddenly broke off the woman.

" Certainly not—how could we have seen him ?"

" Why, he left me to go and 'tend to you."

Annie Abingdon made a sign for their acquaintance to
be cautious. Both the savages were looking up as it
endeavouring to catch the meaning of the conversation.

" What do you s'pose I care for them, umph !" replied
Mrs. Smithson. " That one that I hit with the bag of meal
won't be likely to disturb me again, and the other one
don't amount to anything."

" What time did he leave your house ?"

" It was jest gettin' dark."

" Too late perhaps by a few minutes only."

" Just like him ; I told him to hurry, but he never

would. Pity I married that man ; he always was poor
shucks."

"Your opinion of your husband, Jerusha, hardly
seems to be so good as ours," said Mrs. Abingdon, mildly.

" You don't know him as well as I do," was the logical
reply.

The Indians, it is proper to observe at this point,
evidenced considerable amusement with the words and
actions of the woman who had just come into their
power. True to their nature, they were merciless and
heartless when aroused, but also susceptible, in a slight
degree, to the whimsicality of any transaction. They
stood quietly by while the friends interchanged words. It
was fortunate that one of them knew nothing at all of
the English language, and the other could utter only a
few sentences. Had they comprehended the statement that
old Gershom Smithson had set out to look after the wel-
fare of the Abingdons, it is hardly to be supposed they
would have lingered in such proximity to the settlement.
They seemed to realise that they had secured an original
character, and were content for the time to receive the
amusement she afforded.

Mrs. Smithson sat bolt upright on the horse, with the
sleeping infant upon her breast, without giving the least
heed to her captors, who were paying such assiduous
attention to her. She still held secure the bag of meal,
her chief provision for the journey that she had undertaken.

"Ain't those purty looking critters to stop decent
women like us ?" she exclaimed, looking with the most
supreme disgust toward the two aborigines, blissfully unconscious of this disparaging remark.

" They are repulsive—"

Annie Abingdon paused, for the two individuals had again caught some suspicious sound. They looked off in the darkness, and then one disappeared. The other paused a moment, and then making a warning motion with his knife toward the captives, silently followed.

"I'll warrant Gersh is coming," whispered Mrs. Smithson, as if there was little consolation in the fact. "You might know he hadn't sense enough to keep from making a noise."

CHAPTER XII.

THE DISH OF HASTY-PUDDING.

MRS. SMITHSON was mistaken. The cherished partner of her life, at that moment, was nowhere in the neighbourhood. The precise nature of the disturbing cause none of our friends ever learned. They saw nothing, neither did they hear anything unusual during the absence of their captors. The latter remained so long away that considerable speculation was caused.

"Wonder whether the fools have gone off, and left us?" said Jerusha Smithson. "Jest like 'em."

"Hardly probable," replied Mrs. Abingdon. "It isn't likely they will give us up until they are compelled to do so."

"Do you think your husband is near us?" asked Annie.

"Gracious alive! no. If he was, he would have come stumbling right into us. He wouldn't know enough to sneak around, like anybody else."

"I s'pose George was in the battle?"

"Yes."

"Hain't seen him since?"

"Not since morning."

"Don't know nothin' 'bout him then—whether he's been killed or not ?"

"No; we hope not, but we can only pray for the best."

"If they'd killed my old man, I'd never forgive them. I'd have followed them up as long as I lived."

"You are more fortunate than the rest of the families. There have been many, oh! how many, desolate homes made to-day."

"I know it, and that is what makes me so mad at these critters. I feel just like tearing their eyes out, whenever I look at them."

"I am afraid, Jerusha, if we were in the hands of others, we should be treated a great deal worse than these act toward us."

"I say, Mrs. Abingdon, they've gone away so long, that maybe they don't intend to come back for a long while. Let's leave ! "

"Why can't we ? " whispered Annie to her mother, as she arose to her feet.

"I am afraid they are watching us."

"Don't believe it."

Mrs. Smithson slid down from her horse.

"If we should try to ride away, they'd be sure to hear us. I hate to leave this horse, but Gersh can knock over another savage and take his. So let's walk off in the woods, and how are they to find us when they come back ? "

Mrs. Abingdon and her daughter began seriously to meditate upon the project proposed. They could hear and see nothing of their captors, and if they could once pass beyond the light of the fire, which was already beginning to smoulder, there were strong probabilities **of** their getting safely away.

" It will not do to wait," said Annie, with natural impatience.

" No ; come on," added Mrs. Smithson. " I can walk faster than either of you, if I have a baby to carry."

" I am ready—"

Mrs. Abingdon paused in consternation ; for, chancing to turn her head, she observed one of their hateful captors standing behind a tree scarcely a dozen feet away, watching their every movement. She saw he was ready to spring upon the first one who should attempt to move away, and both she and her daughter knew the temper of the American Indian too well to brave it.

" We are seen," said Mrs. Abingdon, "we have been watched from the beginning."

" Where ? Who ? What do you mean ?"

" Look there !" replied Mrs. Abingdon, motioning to the tree behind which the savage was partially concealed.

" Ain't that mean ? Jest like the critters, listening to what other people are saying."

The savage, finding his presence observed, now came forth and began replenishing the fire.

" Don't he act as if he was ashamed ?" said Mrs. Smithson, surveying him in the most scornful disgust.

" I cannot say that he does, Jerusha," returned Mrs. Abingdon, smiling in spite of herself. " I very much doubt whether he **is** capable of feeling shame, after committing so many crimes.

" If the other one doesn't come purty soon, let's set on to this one. I can manage him, if Mrs. Abingdon will hold on to the baby a little, and Annie will only bite and scratch a bit. She's got temper enough to fight like a wild-cat. Ugh! I can hardly keep my hands off the villain !"

Our lady friends were hardly prepared for the very vigorous project proposed by their companion in captivity. Mrs. Smithson's conduct, in short, showed all too plainly her need of a prudent counsellor. The point beyond which endurance ceases to be a virtue, is very speedily reached when an American Indian is in question, and more than once had she wavered about that point. Both of her captors held in themselves the power of checking her annoyance at any moment when it became too great to bear.

Filled with this thought, the quiet, even-tempered Mrs. Abingdon remonstrated with her.

"Jerusha, suppose one of these Indians should take it into his head to murder you, what would there be to prevent it ?"

The direct question rather startled her.

"Nothing I s'pose ; law suz, what do you mean ?"

"I mean if you are not very careful they will do it. They are somewhat amused at your actions, but if you annoy them too much, they will not wait a moment to kill you."

"Mother is right," added Annie, "although I sometimes allow my indignation to place me in great danger."

"Fudge ; who's afeard ?" snapped Mrs. Smithson.

It was very evident, in spite of this vaunting assertion, that the fiery lady was impressed by the caution so kindly given ; and while her animosity was rather increased than diminished by this truth, she mentally resolved to be a little more gracious in her manner. Old Gershom, if roundly be-rated now and then, still held a warm place in her heart, and the infant, lying all unconscious upon her breast, would unhesitatingly be given the sacrifice of her life, should it become necessary. Placed on the same footing as one of the Indians, no doubt she would have become an exceedingly intractable customer; but it is not necessary to refer to the impossibility of her ever holding this position.

The kindly admonition of Mrs. Abingdon came in good time, for the forbearance of Jerusha was immediately tested. He who had watched the captives with such a suspicious eye now approached her horse and tied him to a sapling, in the same manner that the other one had been secured. Then coming up to Mrs. Smithson, he extended his hand for the bag of meal.

"Let him me—want him."

"Take him, then," she replied, stepping away from her property and allowing him to claim it, instead of reaching it to him.

Unfastening the top, the savage placed his hand in it, and began fumbling with the meal, as if immensely pleased at the soothing sensation it communicated to his hand.

"Ugh—nice—good," he said, drawing forth a handful and placing it in his mouth. It proved hardly so pleasant when manipulated in this manner; and, some of it getting in his nostrils, produced a fit of sneezing more amusing to the by-standers than to himself.

At this juncture, the second Indian made his appearance, bearing a kettle partially full of water. Where he had procured this was a mystery to the captives, and was never explained. Some fugitive fleeing over the Old Warrior's Path may have been plundered by one of the savages, and this taken from him. At any rate, he seemed to have a better idea of the uses of meal than his comrade, for the kettle was intended to receive it, his purpose evidently being to make his supper resemble a civilized one, as much as was possible under the circumstances.

Cutting two large, green, knotty sticks, the Indian pressed them into the ground, one on either side of the fire, and the tops uniting above, so that a strong, enduring support was made for the kettle. This was suspended from the top, and the savage, stepping back, handed the bag to Mrs. Smithson, pointing at the same time significantly toward the fire.

" What does he want?" asked the woman appealed to, not quite certain of his meaning.

" He seems to have so much confidence in your culinary skill as to wish you to prepare him his supper," replied Mrs. Abingdon.

Mrs. Smithson set about carrying out his wishes at once, feeling, in spite of the surrounding circumstances, somewhat flattered that she should be selected for this purpose.

" Let me take care of your baby," added Mrs. Abingdon, approaching and taking the infant from her grasp.

Thus freed from all restraint, the cook began mixing the meal in the water, which was rapidly approaching the boiling point, from the fact that one of the Indians was constantly replenishing the fire.

" I only wish I had a lot of p'ison to put in it," said Mrs. Smithson, glancing toward her friends, as she stirred the pudding with a stick. " They're such pigs they'll eat all of it, and they'd never notice the p'ison till it was too late."

Neither Mrs. Abingdon nor Annie made any response, although the latter was half inclined to join in the vindictive wish just expressed.

When the cook had poured in the quantity of meal she needed, one of the savages made an examination of the bag and discovered the bread and meat in the bottom. Both ate sparingly of it, and then laid it aside, so as not to destroy their appetite for the grand feast which was preparing.

" If I only had a little salt, I would make a dish that you would like," said Mrs. Smithson, addressing herself to the ladies.

" Never mind us—they do not wish for salt, and you must make it to suit them."

" That's the worst of it. I don't believe they know nothin' about pudding, and see if I don't l'arn 'em something."

" You do not intend—you would not— "

Mrs. Abingdon paused, not knowing how to complete the sentence. She gathered from Jerusha Smithson's manner, that she had decided upon some scheme by which to revenge herself—but could not decide upon its precise nature. She was fearful that, by some imprudent act, she would bring the fury of the savages upon the entire party.

" I do hope you will be careful, Jerusha."

" I will—careful—that they catch it," she added, in a tone that none heard but herself.

In the meantime, the meal was fast becoming pudding, and the ravenous aborigines were impatiently waiting for the moment when their enjoyment was to begin.

" How you going to eat it ? " suddenly demanded Mrs. Smithson. " Get some bark to put in on."

More by gestures than anything else, she made one of them comprehend what she meant. The article desired was speedily procured, and she lifted the kettle from the

for the first instalment. She poured out a pint or so of
the beautiful yellow mass, that looked like molten gold,
and they looked up to her for instructions as to how it
should be disposed of.

"What are you waiting for you fools ? Eat it quick
while it is warm !"

Each tipped up his bark, and poured into his open
mouth the fiery mass. Then followed a howl of agony,
as the two spluttered out the scalding stuff, and ran
blindly hither and yon in their torment. The tears were
streaming from eyes that were " unused to weep," and it
may be questioned whether the burning stake would have
wrung such demonstrations from the two victims.

Mrs. Abingdon and Annie could but laugh at the
ludicrousness of the whole scene. Mrs. Smithson, the
author of all this misery, stood looking quietly on, with
an expression that a close observer would have pro-
nounced indicative of a hypocritical commiseration for
their suffering.

CHAPTER XIII.

ON THE PATH.

It required young Arthur Abingdon but a few moments to acquaint his friends with the main facts of the
capture of his mother and sister, and the manner in
which he had eluded their vigilance, and reached home.
Young as he was, he possessed enough prudence to approach the house cautiously. By so doing, he saw the
sentinel first, which certifies to the extreme peril that
personage underwent by his self-appointed duty.

But the most exciting announcement was, that the In-few miles away—proceeding at a leisurely gait—and following a regularly travelled path. Having no reason to fear pursuit, it was not to be expected that they should take any precautions to guard against it.

Old Gershom was smiling grimly, the young Quaker quiet and pleased, while the lieutenant could scarcely restrain himself.

"We shall soon have them!" he exclaimed. "Only two of them! I wouldn't be afraid to attack them, if I was alone."

"Hardly enough to make a decent row—s'pose I contract to take them in hand," said Gershom.

"Thee both are acting in a foolish and unbecoming manner. Thou knowest not what we may have to encounter, and George, if thou cannot restrain thyself, we shall surely be compelled to leave thee behind when we depart."

"Ah! Stoddard, no impatience; you will find me cool enough when the danger comes; but now, when a fellow feels good, what's the use of keeping it to himself?" laughed young Abingdon.

"It is proper for a man to be a man, and not a boy," replied the Friend, unwilling to admit an excuse for such a display of exuberant expectation. The lieutenant was not to be robbed of his good humour, and he therefore laughed and kept silence for the time. Old Gershom, with a happy unconsciousness, did not conceive that a portion of the reproof was intended for him, and his equanimity also remained undisturbed. Arthur, although considerably wearied with his long tramp, was still as eager to join in the pursuit as any of them. Pete simply grinned, and complacently viewed them.

wood, where they halted a few moments to arrange the manner of pursuit.

"Friends," said Franklin, with the deliberation that always characterised him, even at the crisis of danger, "we are about to venture upon an undertaking that is not going to be the child's play that some of thee imagine. Although the captors may now be but two in number, we cannot tell how soon they may increase to a war-party. They may take precautions to guard against capture, and thee all know what care it will require upon our part."

"Jes' de obserwations dat I was goin' to observe," said Pete, eagerly. "I's long been ob de 'pinion dat de part knows for de amount required all know—dat's de fact."

"We can sarcumwent them," said Gershom. "I never yet see'd a white man that couldn't do it when he tried, and if there's any white man that can do it, that same man is Stoddard. Don't you think so, lieutenant?"

"I think he has already proved himself the best Indian fighter in the party."

Not heeding this compliment, which really savoured of the unpalatable, Franklin continued :—

"I will take the lead, as I am acquainted with the Old Warrior's Path, and Gershom will follow. Behind him may come George and Arthur, and last of all, Pete. Pete, dost thou feel qualified to accompany us?"

"'Scuse my modesty, but I's jis' agwine to decline myself for capting, knowin' dat you was likely to make me de leader. I t'inks George will do near as well as me."

"Let there be an end to thy nonsense," admonished Franklin. "I wish to ask thee whether thee thinkest thou can keep silence and obey orders."

"I allers obeys my s'periors, said Pete, addressing his remarks directly to the acknowledged leader.

"If I take the lead," exclaimed Franklin, speaking to those around him, "it is with the distinct understanding that all are to obey me. Gershom has more years than have I, and of him I shall ask advice, when the time comes for counsel."

"Of course, Stoddard, everything is understood. We know our duty. What's the use of waiting?" said the impatient lieutenant.

"My words are chiefly intended for thee, Peter, although not entirely so. Thee will do well to heed them, Peter."

"I will see that he doesn't make a fool of himself."

"I much fear that task was performed for him at his birth," quietly replied Franklin. Pete didn't get a syllable of the meaning of this left-handed compliment, and patiently awaited for any other remarks.

"I mean," said the lieutenant, with marked emphasis, "that any insubordination upon the part of Pete shall be followed by the severest punishment."

Pete understood precisely as much of this as he did of the compliment just referred to. Conceiving that enough had been said for all parties to understand, the young Quaker took the advance, and the little company entered the woods.

Fairly within the gloom of the forest, following the invisible trail that all knew lay beneath their feet, with the certainty that the goal was but a short distance away— strange and unwonted emotions took possession of all. The quiet persevering Friend, who at his Master's beck, would have walked straight up to Death himself, felt a quicker throb of his heart, as he reflected upon his momentous errand. The only female that ever had held dominion in his affections was now in dire extremity, needing the strong arm that was doing its utmost to help her. How his heart thrilled, as he reflected that in all probability the next few hours would decide the matter of life and death.

Similar in some respects, and yet far different in others, were the feelings of the lieutenant. Joyous, hopeful, grateful, he knew he was hastening to the rescue of cherished ones—that was enough. His only desire was to get on—on—on—to strike the desecrating savages to the earth, and set the captives free, and he found it hard to keep time with the measured tread of their imperturbable guide.

The temperament of old Gershom might, in some points, be considered a compromise between that of the lieutenant and the Quaker. Although well advanced in years, he had taken an active part in many of the forays in the Indian country, and he experienced the peculiar thrill of expectation that passes like a shock through the warrior's breast when he realises that he really is upon the eve of battle.

The thought most occupying his mind was the desire that circumstances had been such that Jershua had been the companion of the hapless fugitives. It will be recollected that Arthur made his escape before the capture of the strong-minded woman, and therefore knew nothing about it. It would have been well, had the old man been given a glimpse of his spouse at that particular time.

The Old Warrior's Path, as it was termed for many years before and after the Wyoming massacre, was so well marked, that there was no occasion for our friends going astray. Franklin walked with a sure step, not once looking to the ground, but only ahead, to right and left, ready for the first glimmer of light among the trees.

The first mile, and somewhat more, was passed in entire silence by the party, and without any interruption. The gloom around, the impressive nature of their errand, had sobered all, and each one was wrapped in his own thoughts. Some distance further, the leader paused for a few moments' consultation.

"Since we started," said he, "I have been pondering upon this matter, and have come to the belief that the heathen are not fleeing—that they have encamped, and we may, therefore, look for their camp-fire."

"Precisely my 'pinion—and I was jes' goin' to observe it when you observed it, and saved me the trouble," said Pete, with a flourish.

"What reason have you for thinking thus?" inquired the lieutenant.

"What reason hath thee for supposing otherwise? Why should they flee? After such an utter defeat of the whites in the Valley, need they fear pursuit? When all who have the chance are running away, have they cause to think that any will seek a contest with them?"

These pointed and earnest inquiries answered all questions. Old Gershom and the lieutenant were convinced, although several questions arose in the mind of the latter.

"It would be no hardship for the Indians themselves to travel all night—then why should they show enough consideration for their captives to halt upon their account?"

"If they took them away, they will take care of them, and give them rest when they need it?"

"But, Stoddard, are they not mounted? Could they not ride for hours!"

"They could, but it would be tiresome and dangerous in the woods—"

"Golly gracious! I'm killed!" shouted Pete, in terrified accents.

All were startled, and paused to understand the nature of this new danger. He was heard spitting and spluttering, as if he had suffered some severe injury.

"What's the matter?" demanded the lieutenant, both in curiosity and with considerable anger.

"Noffin' now—all right—stepped out one side de path, and run a big limb under my chin—t'ought I'd sawed my neck off at fust, but b'leve I didn't. Needn't wait any longer fur me."

"If the heathen be anywhere near, thou hast probably warned them, and placed them on their guard against us," said Stoddard Franklin, in his quiet, significant tone.

"Guess dey ain't nowhar' near," returned Pete, with perfect *nonchalance.*

"Another such an occurrence, and thee will not be allowed to accompany us."

Pursuit was once more resumed. All eyes were now occupied in endeavouring to pierce the darkness in quest of the glimmering light that was to betray the whereabouts of the party. Arthur, upon being questioned, gave it as his opinion that they were very near the spot where he gave his captors the slip. As this did not occur until night had fairly set in, there was reason to suppose the Indians themselves were at no great distance. The leader once more admonished silence and caution upon all, and advanced more stealthily, but with the same deliberate activity that had characterised him from the beginning.

It was while hurrying forward in this manner, with that silent expedition which makes the nerves so sensible to the slightest disturbance, that Pete Weldon gave vent to another exclamation, that startled everyone around him.

"Golly gracious! I'm nigh killed dis time, sure. No mistake, I cotched it now !"

The party halted, and in angry silence awaited an explanation. But Pete seemed in no ways disposed to give it, until peremptorily questioned by the lieutenant.

"Wal, you see, I was walking 'long, t'inking ebery t'ing was right, when whack went my feet agen somethin'—dat's all."

"Peter," said Stoddard Franklin, with his invariable gentle voice, "thee knowest the way back, dost thee not?"

"T'inks I does, only got to keep in de path. Ye beginnin' to get scart? If ye bees, I'll show you de way."

"Do thou turn thy face around toward home, and as soon as thou hast done that, begin walking, and do not stop walking so long as thou art near us—or it will not go well with thee."

"But, Massa George—" pleaded the negro.

"Not another word—go !"

Despite the command, Pete was about to remonstrate, when he heard the young man make a step toward him. He understood what this meant, and he hesitated no longer. So fearful, indeed, was he of encountering the dreadful Quaker, that he ran a few steps to make sure of being out of his way.

Franklin listened until his steps were heard no more, and then resumed the pursuit. They progressed in the regular "Indian file," walking quite rapidly, and yet with such silence that they almost might have brushed the face of a sentinel without his even being aware of their presence.

They had advanced something less than half-a-mile

further, when a suppressed exclamation from the leader caused them to halt.

"I saw a light through the trees," he whispered, "but 'tis gone again."

All moved slowly forward a few steps, when an unmistakable glimmer was seen. They were in the vicinity of a camp-fire beyond all question.

CHAPTER XIV

FOOLED.

A SHORT consultation was now held. All believed they were within a few rods of the hostile camp, and that the moment of rescue was close at hand.

"Remain here," said Franklin. "I will steal up to the camp-fire and find out how matters stand. If it be expedient, I will then summon thee to my assistance. Do not leave this place, as I may not know where to look for thee."

"Wouldn't it be better for me to go along?" said young Abingdon, who did not altogether like this remaining behind, when his dear friends might need his presence. "Remember there are two Indians—both armed—rather more than a prudent man would attack single-handed."

"Thee knows me well enough, George, to know that I will not be rash and thoughtless. I go not now to fight but to learn how matters stand. I will rejoin thee before striking a blow."

"Good-bye, then."

The daring young Quaker moved aside in the direction of the camp-fire, while the three friends that he left behind him gathered closely together to wait and listen for his return.

"George," whispered Arthur, after a few moments' silence, "I don't think this is the place where those Indians stopped."

"Why, how do you know anything about it?"

"I think I was mistaken when I said I run away from them back yonder. This looks just like the place."

"All places look alike when it is dark, you know," returned the lieutenant.

"But they all don't look like this," persisted the boy. "There is a big tree right beside us, that I know is the one I hid behind for a few minutes when they were looking for me."

"We have passed a good many large trees, and I am sure you could not tell them apart in the night."

"Maybe I'm wrong, but I don't think so."

"It would be best not to think anything about it."

"George," whispered old Gershom, "if I ain't greatly mistook, there's somebody behind us."

"Have you seen any one?" asked the young man, somewhat startled at the remark.

"No, but I have heard some one—walking very softly, as if they was trying to slip up behind us without our hearing them."

As we have stated, all had stepped aside from the path, and they now kept profound silence. Nothing, however, was heard.

"Perhaps it was Pete coming back," suggested the lieutenant.

"It might be, but I don't think it is. He has probably laid down in the woods and gone to sleep. It sounded to me like the tread of an Indian."

This was rather startling information. If some dusky redskin was pursuing them, it was in his power materially to interfere with the rescue. The utmost care could scarcely guard from a treacherous blow from behind. One savage alone could commit murder and glide away before the blow could be returned.

"I've a knife, and if you say the word, I will finish him," said the old man, with resolution in his voice.

"It would be best to await Stoddard's return. You see a flare-up just now might play the mischief all round."

In the meantime, Stoddard Franklin was making the best of his way toward the camp-fire. He knew how wonderfully acute was the Indian's sense of hearing, and that, although wrapped in slumber, still the inadvertent breaking of a twig would rouse him to instant wakefulness; and, as it was impossible to see his footsteps, he could only hope, by the greatest care, to steal unawares upon the enemy.

When fairly within sight of the fire, he observed that it was smouldering, as though it had been neglected for the last hour or so. Taking a careful survey, he was somewhat surprised to see nothing of any person or animal. Approaching still closer, he narrowly examined the camp. On one side, he finally detected a dark body, strongly resembling a man lying upon the ground. A closer scrutiny revealed still another, and a closer scrutiny nothing more at all.

What meant all this? Where were Annie Abingdon and her mother? Where were the horses upon which they must have ridden? Where were the sentinels that should have been maintaining their vigilant watch?

These were the questions that came to the mind of the young Friend, as he gazed in perplexity upon the camp-fire. There were some persons evidently in his vicinity, and most probably enemies, but of the latter fact there could be no absolute certainty. Everything seemed to indicate that he had come upon the wrong camp.

Before approaching closer, he purposely broke a twig, to ascertain the identity of those stretched upon the ground. He narrowly watched them, but could not detect the slightest movement or sign of life.

This convinced him that the persons before him belonged to his own race, and he boldly approached the fire. On the ground he discovered two men stretched in profound slumber.

"My friends, thee sleep soundly !" he said, shaking one by the shoulder. The person thus disturbed opened his eyes and gazed with a bewildered air around him.

"What's the matter ? What's up, eh ? What did you say ?"

"Thy companion is also asleep. I will arouse him."

Whereupon young Franklin gave him a rather emphatic shaking.

"Strikes me, stranger," said the first mentioned, rather gruffly, "you're taking a good deal on yourself, 'sturbing two respectable gentlemen in this style."

"When thou art gifted with a due amount of prudence, thou wilt thank me for what I have done."

"What's the row ? Let's hear."

The other man by this time was thoroughly awake, and was looking with an inquiring air about him.

"Wert thou in the battle ?"

"We reckon we was," replied the one who had first recovered his consciousness. "Do you see that arm ?" he asked, holding up the bandaged member. "Done by one of them infarnal tomahawks. I got a good whack alongside my head, while Jim didn't git a seratch."

"How didst thou escape ?"

" We made for Forty Fort when we found the day had gone ag'in us; but the dogs headed us off, and so Jim and me took to the woods. We was so tuckered out that we struck a fire, and jis keeled over and went asleep.

" Why did thee kindle a fire ?"

" Wal', we wanted to smoke our pipes by it a while. What's the harm ?"

" I only wonder, my friends," said the Quaker, in his most earnest manner, " that thou hadst not been toma-hawked ere thou had been here a half-hour."

" You don't say so, now! Jim and me had an idea that all the Injins in the States had come down in the Valley. At any rate, we didn't believe there was any in the woods about us."

"There thou art grievously mistaken. A kind Provi-dence above has protected thee thus far; tempt it no further."

To show the earnestness of his words, Stoddard with-drew beyond the circle of light thrown out by the smouldering camp-fire. This simple action was more significant than any words could have been; and the two men followed him with an alacrity that on any other oc-casion would have been ludicrous.

" I am seeking a party of the heathen, who have carried off as prisoners two friends of mine. I took thy camp-fire for theirs."

" You don't say, now, you came alone? That'll hardly go down."

" I have companions a short distance away," returned Franklin, hesitating whether to invite them to join his party or not.

" Do you need any help ?"

" I cannot say that we do. We are more than powerful enough to overcome the heathen whom we are seeking; and while my friends would be all glad to see thee, yet thy presence in our party would hardly add to its efficiency."

"All right, I'm glad to hear it; for the fact is, I am powerful sleepy, and I'm jist going to stretch on the ground out here, where we won't be as likely to be seen, and snooze till morning."

As this seemed to be the inclination of his companion, our friend, after bidding them a kind good-bye and some useful advice, made his way back to where young Abingdon was waiting and wondering at his prolonged absence. His communication, as may well be imagined, was a great disappointment to the fiery lieutenant, who had already cocked his rifle, so as to be ready when the crisis should come.

"Baffled again," he muttered, as he let the hammer of his rifle down. "I had begun to think that maybe you had secured them by stratagem."

"We must press on without delay," suggested old Gershom. "It's gettin' well-nigh into the night, and it's my opine that we won't be able to do much when the daylight is about."

"They must have been a couple of natural-born fools," remarked the lieutenant, alluding to the two men who had been left by the camp-fire.

"Wanting greatly in prudence, we must admit; but we are losing precious time."

They were on the point of resuming their pursuit, when old Gershom whispered: "See here, Stoddard, there's something following us. I heard it just as you came up."

"Has thee heard any noise before?"

"I did, two or three times, and told George about it,

and proposed to go back and git rid of whatever it might
be that was bothering us, but he thought I'd best wait till
you came."

" It may be Peter."

" What I suggested, but Gersh thinks different."

" It don't act like a darkey; it comes up as sly as a cat,
and is then gone before you know it."

" It will not do to go into danger when this enemy is
behind us. He may not only defeat our rescue, but
place our own lives in imminent peril."

" Just my opine exactly, and so, if you've no 'bjection,
here goes for settling the matter at once."

" Dost thou feel able to cope with one of the treacherous heathen ?"

" I feel able 'nough to cope with two of 'em, if there's
anything like fair play."

" Call on God to sustain thee, and make haste."

The words were scarcely uttered, when old Gershom
disappeared as silently as a shadow.

" I fear it may be Peter," remarked Franklin, after
they had listened a moment.

" And so do I. If so, it will be rather dangerous for
the fellow, for Gershom is a tough and wiry opponent."

" He will not strike until sure whether it is an enemy
or a friend."

" He may feel sure that it is an enemy, and therefore
not take the trouble to inform himself with absolute certainty."

" If that be the case, I shall recall him."

" Hold !" admonished the lieutenant. " No harm will
result from this, I feel confident."

Some fifteen or twenty minutes passed silently away,
when both Franklin and Abingdon were impatient. A

short time later, and the former gave a low whistle, as a signal for Gershom to rejoin them. In a moment he appeared beside him.

"Heard him two, three times," he whispered, "but I couldn't get a sight of him. 'Fraid he heard me."

"We have no more time to lose, but must press on. It will—"

"Hist !" exclaimed the old man, "there he is again !"

As he spoke, he darted backward, and the next moment came a short struggle, followed by a heavy fall.

"Now I've got you ! Say your prayers mighty quick !"

"Don't, don't ! massa Gershom ! It's me, Pete ! I won't hurt you if you don't hurt me ! Golly gracious ! you's choking !"

The revelation apparently came at the critical moment, for the edge of the cold steel was already felt by the prostrate and terrified negro. Smithson released him, muttering, "Jes' in time to save you."

No one in that little party suspected, what was the truth, that the old man knew from the beginning that it was Pete Weldon who was following them, and with a characteristic sort of grim humour, he took this plan of thoroughly frightening him.

CHAPTER XV

ON THE WAY AGAIN.

PETE WELDON was so humble and penitent—so frightened and earnest in his promises to obey all commands, and maintain absolute silence—that Franklin agreed to allow him to accompany them.

"Wouldn't 've come back ag'in, but I found dar's so many Injins blocked up my way, dat I t'ought I'd go round! So I started back to come out of de oder end ob de path, when I overtuck you."

"Let us hear no word from thee until thou art questioned, as we have no objections to thy company."

"All right, dat's what I t'ought. You won't hear nuffin from me—dat's mighty sart'in, till you axes, for if dar's one t'ing dat dis chile eber knowed, it was to keep his mouf shut when nobody didn't want to hear him not say nuffin. Missis Abingdon and Annie will bofe tell ye de same, if ye axes 'em, and if dey only t'ink about it, dey'll tell ye without axing. If you's a mind—"

"There, keep still, Pete!" interrupted the lieutenant. "You have said enough to last till morning."

"Yah! yah! t'ink so, does yees?"

"I hain't had any practice on any Injin very lately," said old Gershom, "and I'd like to get my hand in. So if Pete here talks too much, just say the word, and I'll stop him so well, he'll never say anything more."

This had the effect of quieting the loquacious negro for the time. The lieutenant and Quaker exchanged a few words in an undertone, and then the little party moved on through the gloom of the forest in their determined quest for their friends.

By this time it had come to be a doubtful question with both the young men, whether the Indians had really encamped or not. It might be, they reflected, that they had paused, but had doubtless resumed their flight, and perhaps at that moment were miles distant.

The lieutenant could not help believing that the escape of little Arthur had opened their eyes to a threatened danger. He would be sure to make his way back to the house, where if none of his friends presented themselves, they would be hunted out, and the probabilities were, that a pursuit would have been organized at that very moment. The Indians might have been justified in believing that until morning at least they were safe from disturbance; but it was not characteristic of their race that they should make no provision against it.

Stoddard Franklin, as he cautiously led the way over the Big Warrior's Path, occupied his mind with all manner of conjectures and speculations. To him, every phase of the captivity presented itself. His friends might be tomahawked, although this was extremely improbable. Their captors might have taken the alarm from the flight of Arthur, and be hurrying them mercilessly forward, subjecting them to every possible indignity of which the mind can conceive. Should this be the truth, there is no stating how fearful the retribution of the quiet Friend would prove. The manner in which he clenched his hands, and closed his teeth when this thought presented itself, certainly augured ill for any guilty ones who might come into his power—and again, should he find that Annie and her mother had received kind treatment at the hands of the savages, the latter were certainly safe from his vengeance.

Hopeful and confident, the little band of pursuers were threading their way through the forest, when their progress was checked by an occurrence that was natural and was yet unexpected by all. Young Arthur who had gone bravely through numerous trials, now began to understand that his frame was overtasked. He was a delicate boy, entirely unaccustomed to fatigue, his will, unduly stimulated by the extraordinary circumstances, having sustained him thus far. It had not escaped the attention of Lieutenant Abingdon that his young brother had been lagging ever since the last halt.

When his fatigue became painfully manifest, he spoke:
"Getting tired, Arthur?"

"Yes; I must sit down and rest," he wearily replied.
"I cannot go any further."

Franklin overheard the reply, and paused.

"We have never thought we were taxing thy strength
too severely. We should have remembered it."

"What is to be done, Stoddard?"

"We must allow him to take a good rest."

"But the time that will be lost?"

"Cannot be a great deal. It belongs to the boy, and
we cannot withhold it."

"I makes dis yer prop'sition," said Pete. "Yer leave
Massa Arthur here, under charge of Mr. Smithson and
de leftenner, while me and Massa Stoddard go on to hunt
de Injins. If yer gits scart, why you jes' holler, and
we'll come back. When we gets sight ob de Injins I'll
set up a yell, so you'll come up, and we'll all jine togever
and make a rush on 'em. If Arthur am tired, ye can
carry him, and make good use ob him too."

"In what manner?" inquired the lieutenant, who felt
a little curiosity to know the plan of the negro.

"Jes' took him up to de fire, and frow him down, so
dat his heels would hit de Injins on de head, and den,
you see, his weight will hold 'em down while we take de
wimmin and runs away. Yah! yah! but dat will come
it ober dem."

Pete seemed to imagine his plan an admirable one, for
he laughed heartily, restraining any noise in doing so as
much as possible.

When the halt was made, the subject of it had
stretched himself upon the ground, where he was enjoying
to the utmost his relief from exertion.

" Arthur has my entire pity," remarked Franklin, in a sympathizing tone ; " his frame cannot undergo the exertion that we do not feel. We should have given him the rest he needs, long since."

" See here," said old Gershom, who had listened to the remarks of all. " He is but a lad, why cannot I pick him up and carry him? I've an idea them Indians ain't fur off, and we're losing mighty precious time by waiting here. They may get wind of our being on the trail, and give us the slip, after all."

" It will require but a few moments for Arthur to recover himself, and we can then resume our pursuit."

" Yes, you needn't wait long for me," said the boy. " I'm nearly rested now."

" Do you believe, Stoddard, the Indians have really encamped?" asked young Abingdon, now that a few minutes were left for conversation.

" I think they have, and yet I do not feel so sure of it as I did an hour ago. It may be that the heathen are anxious to get away from the Valley as soon as possible, and will therefore lose no time that they are not compelled to lose."

" If such be the case, it is going to be no easy matter to overtake them. We shall have to leave Arthur along the way, and make better time ourselves."

" They will not travel rapidly, for it will be impossible, while darkness lasts, but when morning comes, they can press forward with considerable rapidity."

" We must recollect, too, that they have a good start of us, and even if they travel slowly, it must take us considerable time to come up with them."

" If it were daytime, we might look for something to direct us. As they have horses, the trail of the party cannot be concealed, and besides, Annie and her mother have shrewdness enough to give us a sign now and then, if there be any—"

"I don't know about that, Stoddard. These Indians are the most cunning and treacherous people in the world. They would keep a sharp eye to the doings of their captives, and anything like that would be sure to be seen."

"It might be seen, George, but what of it? Suppose a limb were broken, it would be a guiding finger to us—one that could not be destroyed."

"It seems to me it would be too dangerous for them to repeat, at any rate."

"It might be dangerous, I can well see—that is, if our friends should be seen repeating it, after they had been forbidden. But the eyes of the heathen could not well be upon them continually, and I much mistake the character of Annie if anything they say or do could deter them."

"If her temper should be aroused, no Indian could quell it. It is fortunate for her that she has the companionship of her mother, who can restrain and direct her.'

"A kind and gentle hand can mould Annie to any purpose that may not be wrong."

"You have hope, then, of accomplishing that?" laughed young Abingdon.

"I am certain," replied the lover, in the most serious of voices.

"She will do anything for mother, and she will do still more for you—if such an expression be allowable."

The Quaker said nothing, but the lieutenant was never more certain of anything in the world than that he passed his hand to his face and brushed a tear from his eye. Quiet and undemonstrative as he was, there were deep fountains in his breast which could be stirred by the sight of pain and suffering. More than once, on that dark night of the great Wyoming massacre, as he threaded his way through the gloom of the wilderness, the tears trickled down his cheeks, and he could have wept aloud. One of the most prominent characteristics of his nature was an iron will, and, if necessary, he could hold in subjection these powerful emotions—could wear a calm, placid face, when all within was surging with feeling. Here, where he believed no human eye could see him, he did not strive to keep back the tears that welled up.

"I'm rested!" exclaimed Arthur, springing to his feet. "You needn't wait any longer."

"Rest thyself sufficiently, so as not to become fatigued again very soon."

"Oh, I could travel fifty miles!" was the characteristic reply of the boy. His "second strength" had come to him.

"Den it am my 'pinion dat if you's able to walk fifty miles, you has de 'bility to walk forty-nine, and as I don't t'ink de Injins am dat fur away, den what am de 'sessity ob waitin' any longer? Dat am Pete's 'pinion."

"Has anyone requested thy opinion, Peter?" asked Franklin, in his quiet, significant manner.

"Doesn't know as dar' has. Simply wolunteered it, without bein' axed, dat's all."

"After this, wait until thou art asked for thy opinion."

"Dat's de way I allers does, 'cept when dey don't ax it, den I don't wait, but gibs it without axin.'"

A moment later the pursuers were on their way, advancing in Indian file, and with the same caution that had characterized their former movements. They had not gone more than the eighth of a mile, when, to the surprise of all, a bright light was seen glimmering among the trees on their right—evidence unmistakable that they were in the vicinity of another camp-fire.

A halt was instantly made, and, as before, it was agreed that the young Quaker should go forward and reconnoitre. This time he took the precaution to carry Lieutenant Abingdon's rifle. Admonishing them not to change their position, and on no account to make any noise, he took his departure like a shadow.

The minutes wore slowly away to those in watching. They endeavoured to keep patience, but, where all were so anxious, it was about impossible. At the termination of what seemed a half-hour, but what in reality was ten minutes, they became conscious that the Friend was among them.

"We have verily found the heathen at last!" were his first words, uttered in the quiet tones that always characterized him.

CHAPTER XVI.

NOW, MY FRIENDS!

"THE heathen have no fears of pursuit," continued the young Quaker; "both are sound asleep."

"And mother and Annie?" asked young Abingdon, all excitement and anxiety.

"Are also asleep — reposing as quietly, to all appearance, as if they were safe in the shelter of their own house. Moreover, there is another with them—"

"An Indian?"

"A woman—wrapped up in a blanket, so that I could not discern her face. I saw the forms of three prisoners stretched upon the ground."

" Are they bound, or secured in any way ?"

" They are tied together by means of cords that are fastened to one of the heathen—so it is impossible for them to stir without awaking their captors."

" I should think they might cut the cords."

" If they had the means ; but the heathen are too shrewd to allow them the opportunity."

" It is fortunate, at any rate, that they have no fears of disturbance. Now, Stoddard, what is the course of action ?"

" Gershom, what is thy advice ?"

" I go for creeping onto 'em unawares like, and then going in promiscuously and smashing them. We've got two loaded rifles, and it ain't likely either one of 'em will miss to-night."

" And what does thou counsel, George ?"

" The suggestion of Gersh strikes me as being as good as anything that I can propose."

" I cannot coincide with thee," returned the Friend, after a moment's pause. " The two heathen seem to have treated the captives with great leniency, and we cannot, therefore, justify ourselves in taking their lives."

" But what can we do under the circumstances ?"

" Take them prisoners ; or, if it be necessary, slay them. But smite them not until we are compelled to do so."

" Give us your entire plan, Stoddard, and let it be executed within the next two minutes."

" Peter will remain here with Arthur—"

" Jes' what I's goin' to s'gest, or else let you all stay here, while I creeps up and finishes dem in skientific style."

" Peter will remain here with Arthur, and make no

noise. All three of us will creep carefully toward the camp-fire. Gershom, who has experience in this kind of business, will cut the cord that binds our friends to the heathen, while George and I will attend to securing them."

"My idea exactly!" exclaimed old Gershom, excitedly. "I will do it so nicely, that none of them will even suspect what I am doin'.

Having decided upon their plan of attack, no further time was wasted in its execution. An additional admonition was given to Peter and Arthur, and then the three began their stealthy approach to the Indian camp-fire.

Old Gershom possessed more skill than either of his companions, and unconsciously to himself advanced more rapidly than they. As a matter of course, he reached the spot first. Both the Quaker and lieutenant called to him in a whisper to wait, but he did not hear them, and they durst not repeat it, for fear of awaking the savages.

The old man crept carefully up to the camp-fire with knife in hand. Reaching forward, with one clear cut he severed the connecting cord. Then, as he turned to the woman lying nearest, he saw with surprise that she was his own wife, Jerusha. Placing his hand upon her shoulder, he gave a gentle shake. Neither she nor the infant stirred. Another more violent shake, and she opened her eyes.

"My dear Jerusha—"

Whack! came the flat of her hand against the side of her husband's head.

"You old fool, what you waking me for? 'Purty time of night for you to come home."

"But, my dear Jerusha—"

"Shet up!"

And the indignant spouse, blissfully unconscious of the surrounding circumstances, turned her back upon him, and addressed herself more assiduously to slumber.

At this juncture, one of the Indians raised his head, and with a startled look gazed about him. At the same instant, he was seized with a grip of iron from behind.

"Verily, my friend, it becometh me to impose restraint upon thee," said Stoddard Franklin, proceeding to secure his arms. The savage, who did not dream that any mercy or quarter would be shown him, struggled so violently that it was almost impossible to secure him. He looked upon the thing as a death-struggle, and became furious in his resistance.

"I much regret the force which I am driven to use," said the Quaker, giving him a blow with his fist that stretched him out limp and senseless as a rag. It required but a few moments then to make a prisoner of him.

Young Abingdon was hardly as prompt in springing upon his adversary, so that the latter, although taken considerably by surprise, was still prepared in a measure for him. He made an attempt to draw his knife, but was borne to the earth before he could do so. The savage was agile and powerful, and it was not long before the lieutenant found he had grappled a man who was every way worthy of him. What would have been the ultimate result of the contest it is hard to say, had not the iron-muscled Quaker interposed.

"Thou art proving thyself exceedingly troublesome," he remarked," and I must perforce act somewhat violently toward thee."

Saying which, he dealt the Indian a blow that stunned him completely, and then quickly secured him.

So silently and rapidly had these incidents taken place, that neither Annie Abingdon nor her mother was awakened. Jerusha Smithson, after turning upon her side, had heard the brief struggle, and turning back again comprehended at a glance her situation, and the situation of her friends.

"Mrs. Abingdon, wake up! Annie, wake up!" she shouted. "They've come! they've come!"

Mother and daughter aroused themselves at the same moment. George Abingdon rushed forward, and fell upon his mother's neck.

"God be praised!" exclaimed the parent, fervently. "God be praised! you are alive and well! And Stoddard is with you!"

The young Quaker had walked forward, and knelt beside Annie, who had risen to the sitting position, and throwing his arms around her, drew her head to his bosom. He did not seek to keep back the tears that would force themselves down his cheeks. For a few moments neither spoke, and then she murmured:—

"How kind God has been! He has spared us all. Not one harmed—all safe. Were you in the battle, Stoddard?"

"Verily, the spirit moved me, and the flesh is weak!"

"Strikes me that your flesh was pretty powerful to-day. Do you see those two Indians lying there? He knocked each of them stiff. We were on Monocacy Island at dusk to-night, and one of the red-skins came at me with his knife, when Stoddard there slipped up behind him, and gave him a blow that tumbled him a dozen feet."

"My dear Jerusha, how came you here?" inquired Gershom, when there was a momentary lull.

" Came on my horse ; don't you know nothin' ?   How should I come ! "

" But I thought you started for Stroudsburg."

" So I did, and so did these nasty Indians, and they cotched me."

" How's the baby ? "

" Well 'nough.   I'm glad you come, for now you can 'tend her till we get to Stroudsburg."

Whereupon, Mrs. Smithson deposited her offspring in the lap of her spouse, and busied herself about other matters.   This awakened the infant, which began a terrific yelling, kicking and scratching, while the father rocked backward and forward upon the ground, in vain attempts to quiet it.

The outcries of the infant convinced the waiting and listening Pete Weldon that it was now safe to make his appearance, and he accordingly came rushing forward.

" Whar's dem Injins ?   Why didn't you call me ?   I want to smash 'em.   Dar' dey am, eh ? "

Seeing they were bound and helpless, he rushed up with the intention of pommeling them, when the Quaker interfered.

" Don't thee touch them, or I will tie thee to one of them, and let thee have it out with him."

" Golly gracious ! I won't," replied the negro, terrified at the bare thought.   " I see dey is fastened, so it wouldn't be hon'rable ! "

Mrs. Smithson busied herself in piling brush upon the fire, so that in a few minutes it was roaring and crackling, and throwing a cheerful light far into the surrounding gloom.   A slight investigation proved that the horses were undisturbed ; and as everyone realised the import-ance of expedition in the matter, preparations were made for resuming the flight of the fugitives from the vicinity of the ill-fated Wyoming Valley.

" What do you intend doing with these Indians ?" inquired Lieutenant Abingdon.

" First we will ascertain how they have treated Annie and her mother. Have they been cruel toward thee ?"

" They have shown far more kindness than we had reason to expect," replied Mrs. Abingdon.

" Have they offered thee insult ?"

" None at all," answered Annie.

" They offered no violence in taking thee prisoners ?" continued the Quaker.

" No ; we have been much disappointed at the treatment we have received at their hands. Had they been civilized beings, we could not have expected much better treatment."

" Still they have taken part in the Wyoming massacre, they are the sworn enemies of our race, and I go for knocking them on the head," replied the fiery lieutenant, who experienced some discomfort from his recent struggle with the Indian, and whose vindictiveness may thereby be partly accounted for.

" Yes ; smash 'em, that's my motto," called out old Smithson.

" Don't you open your mouth ag'in," commanded Mrs. Smithson. " You tend to the baby, that's all you've got to do."

" Yes, my dear Jerusha."

" It does not become us to entertain revenge toward these heathen," pursued the Quaker. " They had the power to do incalculable harm to their captives, but refrained. When one's life depends upon it, perhaps—perhaps resistance may be justifiable."

" Don't say perhaps, Stoddard, for you showed no hesitation to-day."

" It becometh us, therefore, as Christian men, to allow them to go in peace. We cannot murder them, and we have no occasion to hold them as prisoners."

" Why not make prisoners of them, and take them into Stroudsburg ? "

The Quaker shook his head.

" They would be torn to pieces. We will disarm them, and allow them to go."

The subjects of this conversation lay upon the ground, their stoical faces unmoved, and their dark, baleful eyes asking no pity or consideration. Having decided in his own mind what to do, our hero walked up to the prostrate men, drew their knives and tomahawks from their belts, and handed their guns to his friends. Severing their bonds, he then permitted them to rise.

" Now, my heathen friends—"

Both had whisked away like a flash of lightning.

Stroudsburg was yet a goodly distance away, and the passage thereto was encompassed by much danger. Young Arthur Abingdon was mounted upon the horse with Mrs. Smithson ; Annie and her mother were placed upon their own animal, while Gershom took turns with the others in riding the third, and the little party set forth. The men were now provided with rifles and well armed otherwise, so that they had good reason for confidence in themselves. Still they had precious ones in charge, and the anxiety of all was to avoid a collision with any of the dusky denizens of the wood.

All night long the flight was continued. At daylight a short halt was made, and a hasty meal partaken, and when the sun was up they were fairly under way again.

Our friends had the advantage of being in advance of that stream of terror-stricken fugitives that crowded the avenues of escape to Wind Gap and Stroudsburg. The latter place was reached in due time, and devout thanks were returned to God for the beneficent kindness he had shown in leading the little party safe away from the dreadful doom that settled down upon the Westmoreland, on that historical 3rd of July, 1778.

Every exertion was made by the officers and men to restrain the Indians, and many persons and buildings escaped destruction. Among the latter was the Abingdon mansion. After the storm of war had passed, Major Abingdon and his son, the lieutenant, returned to their pleasant home in the Valley. A short distance away was the residence of the young Quaker and his wife. The former had not lost caste among his creed by his brief but eventful part in the invasion of the Valley; and to-day, among his descendants, no name is mentioned with more veneration than that of Stoddard Franklin, the Quaker Scout of Wyoming Valley.

THE END.

LONDON: W. J. JOHNSON, PRINTER, 121, FLEET STREET.

ROUTLEDGE'S SHILLING NOVELS.

By J. FENIMORE COOPER.

In fcp. 8vo, fancy covers, 1s. each.

THE PILOT.
THE PIONEERS.
THE DEERSLAYER.
LIONEL LINCOLN.
THE BRAVO.
THE TWO ADMIRALS.
THE WATERWITCH.
WYANDOTTE.
MILES WALLINGFORD.
THE PRAIRIE.
THE HEATHCOTES.
PRECAUTION.
MARK'S REEF.
THE LAST OF THE MOHICANS.
THE SPY.
THE PATHFINDER.
THE RED ROVER.
THE HEIDENMAUER.
SATANSTOE.
AFLOAT AND ASHORE.
EVE EFFINGHAM.
THE HEADSMAN.
HOMEWARD BOUND.
THE SEA LIONS.
OAK OPENINGS.
NED MYERS.

GEORGE ROUTLEDGE & SONS, Broadway, Ludgate Hill

ROUTLEDGE'S SHILLING NOVELS.

By W. HARRISON AINSWORTH.

WINDSOR CASTLE.

THE MISER'S DAUGHTER.

THE TOWER OF LONDON.

CRICHTON.

JAMES THE SECOND.

OLD ST. PAUL'S.

THE FLITCH OF BACON.

GUY FAWKES.

THE LANCASHIRE WITCHES.

MERVYN CLITHEROE.

OVINGDEAN GRANGE.

ROOKWOOD.

ST. JAMES'S; OR, THE COURT OF QUEEN ANNE.

THE SPENDTHRIT.

THE STAR CHAMBER.

AURIOL.

JACK SHEPPARD.

GEORGE ROUTLEDGE & SONS, Broadway, Ludgate Hill

ROUTLEDGE'S SHILLING NOVELS.

By CAPTAIN MARRYAT.

In fscp. 8vo, fancy covers, 1s. each.

PETER SIMPLE.

JACOB FAITHFUL.

NEWTON FORSTER.

THE PACHA OF MANY TALES.

PERCIVAL KEENE.

JAPHET IN SEARCH OF A FATHER.

FRANK MILDMAY.

MR. MIDSHIPMAN EASY.

THE POACHER.

VALERIE.

THE KING'S OWN.

RATTLIN THE REEFER.

THE PHANTOM SHIP.

THE DOG FIEND.

MISCELLANEOUS.

1s. each.

NOTHING BUT MONEY. By T. S. ARTHUR.

THE FAMILY FEUD. By THOMAS COOPER.

ADELAIDE LINDSAY. By the Author of "EMILIA WYNDHAM."

THE LITTLE WIFE. By Mrs. GREY.

RITA: An AUTOBIOGRAPHY.

LILLY DAWSON. By Mrs. CROWE.

THE HENPECKED HUS-BAND. By LADY SCOTT.

WHOM TO MARRY. By MAYHEW.

TOUGH YARNS. By the "OLD SAILOR."

GEORGE ROUTLEDGE & SONS, Broadway, Ludgate Hill.

LORD LYTTON'S WORKS.

CHEAP EDITION, in fscp. 8vo, Boards,

Price 2s. each.

A STRANGE STORY.

WHAT WILL HE DO WITH IT? Vol. 1.

WHAT WILL HE DO WITH IT? Vol. II.

PELHAM.

PAUL CLIFFORD.

EUGENE ARAM.

THE LAST DAYS OF POMPEII.

THE LAST OF THE BARONS.

RIENZI.

ERNEST MALTRAVERS.

ALICE.

NIGHT AND MORNING.

THE DISOWNED.

DEVEREUX.

THE CAXTONS.

MY NOVEL. Vol. I.

MY NOVEL. Vol. II.

LUCRETIA.

HAROLD.

Price 1s. 6d. each.

GODOLPHIN. | ZANONI.

Price 1s. each.

THE PILGRIMS OF THE RHINE.

LEILA; OR, THE SIEGE OF GRANADA.

GEORGE ROUTLEDGE & SONS, Broadway, Ludgate Hill.

JAMES GRANT'S NOVELS.

Price 2s. each, in Fancy Boards.

THE ROMANCE OF WAR; or, The Highlanders in Spain.

THE AIDE-DE-CAMP.

THE SCOTTISH CAVALIER.

BOTHWELL.

JANE SETON; or, The Queen's Advocate.

PHILIP ROLLO.

LEGENDS OF THE BLACK WATCH.

MARY OF LORRAINE.

OLIVER ELLIS; or, The Fusiliers.

LUCY ARDEN; or, Hollywood Hall.

FRANK HILTON; or, The Queen's Own.

THE YELLOW FRIGATE.

HARRY OGILVIE; or, The Black Dragoons.

ARTHUR BLANE.

LAURA EVERINGHAM; or, The Highlanders of Glenora.

THE CAPTAIN OF THE GUARD.

LETTY HYDE'S LOVERS.

CAVALIERS OF FORTUNE.

SECOND TO NONE.

THE CONSTABLE OF FRANCE.

The above in Cloth Gilt, 2s. 6d. each.

GEORGE ROUTLEDGE & SONS, Broadway, Ludgate Hill.